After the film, there was a news feature showing the Germans bombing sad little villages in Vietnam, and there were also some pictures of Russian scientists and spacemen helping to build the missile bases on the moon.

At the end of the show, the lights went on and Queen Victoria stood in the royal box. Then the orchestra played God Save the Queen, and everyone stood very still.

Michael was tired. Tremendously excited and tremendously tired. He almost fell asleep on the bicycle on the way home. His head ached with excitement. But later, when he was trying to sleep, his head ached for a different reason. He felt that, during the course of the evening, he had discovered something important.

But he didn't know what it was.

The Overman Culture

Edmund Cooper

CORONET BOOKS
Hodder Paperbacks Ltd., London

Copyright © 1971 by Edmund Cooper
First published by Hodder and Stoughton Ltd, 1971
Coronet edition 1974

Printed in Great Britain
for Coronet Books, Hodder Paperbacks Ltd.,
St. Paul's House, Warwick Lane, London, EC4P 4AH
by Richard Clay (The Chaucer Press), Ltd.,
Bungay, Suffolk.

ISBN 0 340 17860 4

Time present and time past
Are both perhaps present in time future,
And time future contained in time past.

T. S. ELIOT

PROLOGUE

Mr. and Mrs. Faraday had a nice little house in Bucking-ham Palace Road, London. They had a nice little rose garden and a nice little pond which contained goldfish. They had colour television and wireless; and they watched the American expedition touch down on Mars, and they listened to Mr. Henry Hall's dance band music. Their house had a nice bay window, where two potted aspidistras flourished, and through which Mr. and Mrs. Faraday sometimes glimpsed Queen Victoria riding in her hover-car or Sir Winston Churchill strolling to the Palace.

They had nice furniture, a tape recorder, a box camera, an electronic cooker and two splendid bicycles. They sometimes went to the pictures on Saturday evening, and they listened to the war news every day.

And they had a little boy called Michael. This is his story. This is how he grew up and eventually discovered the truth.

But when he saw the bodies, chilled beyond death,

beyond life, as they had existed throughout the limbo of millennia; and when he heard the voice say THIS IS MANKIND, he found the truth almost too terrible to bear . . .

ONE

Michael had a good memory. He remembered things significant and insignificant. He remembered—if hazily—when he was young enough to be fed milk only. He remembered the odd child who disappeared from play school, and he remembered the other child who fell (or was pushed?) from the high window and lay all smashed and crumpled on the ground, but not bleeding. And he remembered how he had wanted to know about words, how you could keep them, how you could fix them—perhaps like a drawing—for ever.

He remembered nightmares and fantasies and a growing sense of oddness. He remembered when he first began to hope that people would hurt themselves a little so that he could see if they would bleed. He remembered the questions that did not seem to be properly answered. He remembered that Mother and Father had never ever raised their voices. He remembered his first walk by the River Thames, his first visit to the cinema, his first knowledge of air raids. He remembered when desire first stirred in his flesh, and when he began to love Emily Brontë.

Sometimes he thought he was mad. Sometimes he thought he was sane. Then he began to think he could be both sane and mad ...

It had always been Mother who gave him milk from the bottle. He was sure of that. Always Mother. Always the same kind of smile. Sometimes, particularly when he was tired, drifting in the twilight between waking and sleeping, he could see her face now as it must have seemed then— vast, calm, pleasant, filling half the world.

Mother had always been calm, Mother always was calm, Mother always would be calm. And, for reasons that he could not understand, that, too, seemed terrible.

Father was different. Father was a bit abrupt—stern, even. He always had been, always would be.

Sometimes, Mother and Father laughed. Chiefly, they seemed to laugh when Michael asked silly questions. Michael did not know why the questions were silly. But Father said they were; and so, for a time, he thought they must be.

Later, there were the bigger questions, leading in the end to the biggest question of all.

Where does childhood end and maturity begin? Where do dreams border with reality? Where does truth separate from fantasy? These were problems that haunted Michael. They had been haunting him a long time, long before he had the words to describe them clearly. Before the bricks were abandoned in the nursery, before he rejected the talking teddy-bear because somehow he knew it was a traitor.

Early memories, early dreams. Early delights, early nightmares. The Thames was beautiful and blue, and on a spring morning a small boy could sit on the Embankment wall, staring down through the clear water at shoals of trout playing hide and seek among boulders and waterweed. The sun was warm and the sky hazy; and even with the sounds of war bumping and crumping and thudding away on the other side of the force field, London was sweetly silent. The Sunday silence was best of all. Somehow it seemed to throb.

"What is a force field, Father?"

"That's a big question for a little boy . . . See, the swans are chasing the trout. Do you think they will catch any?"

"The swans aren't chasing the trout, Father. The swans are just floating. The trout don't like moving shadows . . . What is a force field?"

"Michael, there are some things you can't properly understand. A force field is something you can't see, but it is like a big umbrella. We live under it, and even if the laser batteries can't destroy the enemy missiles, they still won't get through the force field. Shall we walk home, now? I think it might rain."

"Yes, Father."

Father was very good at predicting the weather. Amazingly good.

Mother had an electric sewing machine. She liked to make things, and she made almost all of Michael's clothes; but the strange thing was that she seemed to prefer to do most of the sewing by hand. She liked embroidery, and she liked to sit in the evening listening to the wireless—the Palm Court orchestra, or the Beatles, or Nelson Eddy and Jeanette Macdonald—with her needle in her hand.

There was one particular piece of embroidery that Michael remembered. It was to be a new bed quilt for him, covered with lots of small silky animals. It took a long time to complete. For several nights Michael watched his mother working on the shape of an elephant. Each night she seemed to be having to embroider again a part that she had done on a previous night.

Michael was curious. He wondered if she could not see too well by lamp light. He wondered if, in daylight, she would examine her work, be dissatisfied with it and unpick the stitches.

At last, he asked her about it. But she only laughed. "What a quaint little boy you are, Michael. I don't think you can have been watching me very carefully. Of course I don't unpick the stitches when you are at play school. That would be silly."

But thereafter, the bed quilt progressed at a faster rate.

Mother had golden hair, Father had light brown hair, Michael had black hair. One day he asked his parents why this should be so.

Father answered. "It just happens that way, Michael. That is the way it is. Hair comes in different colours like noses come in different shapes and lengths. No two things or people are ever exactly the same. Remember that. It is important ... And Michael. You ask a lot of questions. It shows you are clever. But people can be too clever, and then they get unhappy. Happiness is a great thing, Michael. Happiness and contentment. That is what we want you to have. We want you to lead a happy life. So, don't worry your head with too many questions. It is much more important to enjoy yourself. Now run outside and play for a while, then you will be really tired, and you will sleep well and not have any more of those silly nightmares."

But Michael remembered that the child at play school who fell from the high window and lay all smashed without bleeding had yellow hair. And he remembered that the little girl who fell on her knees in the playground and cried when the blood came had black hair.

And he knew that he liked her very much. And he wondered if it was because she could bleed.

Michael could bleed. Secretly, he would occasionally cut himself a little to make sure he could still bleed. Vaguely, he was afraid that one day he might change. He was afraid that one day he might find no blood left inside him.

TWO

Michael liked being at play school better than he liked being at home. And that was another thing that puzzled him. He felt he should have wanted to be with Mother and Father more.

Play school was a big house in Hyde Park. Every day—except, of course, on Saturday and Sunday—Mother took Michael to school on her bicycle. All the mothers took their children to school on bicycles.

There were lots of children at play school. Some had golden hair, some had brown hair, some had black hair. Some could bleed if they hurt themselves. Michael liked the children who could bleed best of all.

One day he asked a golden-haired child called Virginia if she ever cut herself. Virginia shook her head and ran away, laughing.

Later, Miss Nightingale came and talked to Michael by himself while the other children were sleeping after lunch. Miss Nightingale was very pretty. She had brown hair.

"Michael, why did you ask Virginia Woolf if she ever cut herself?"

"It was a joke, Miss Nightingale."

"It doesn't sound like a joke, Michael. Do you ever cut yourself?"

"No," he lied.

"Why should you want to ask her that?"

Again he lied. "I don't know."

Miss Nightingale smiled. "Never mind. The most important thing is to be happy, Michael. Strange ideas can make people unhappy. Try to be like the other children."

"Yes, Miss Nightingale."

"Go to sleep, now. This afternoon we shall have a picnic tea in the park, and we shall play some exciting games, and we shall all be happy."

"Yes, Miss Nightingale. Thank you."

Michael's best friends were Horatio Nelson, Ernest Rutherford, Jane Austen and Emily Brontë. At one time or another, he had seen them all bleed—even if only a little.

Play school was pleasant, but sometimes it could be boring. There was drawing and painting, and acting and singing, and games and sleeping. The teachers told stories, the children told stories, and there were walks in the park.

But most of all, Michael wanted to ask questions. But there never seemed to be much time for questions, because the teachers were always busy organizing some activity or sharing out the toys or putting out the paints; and the children were busy being children, busy being happy by not asking questions. Most of them had already decided that questions were a waste of time. Sooner or later, they thought, they would learn about important things just naturally. Like they learned how to do lots of things that would make them happy but tired, so that they would sleep without having bad dreams.

Michael had bad dreams. He did not tell Mother and Father about them any more. Bad dreams made Mother and Father think that he was not tired enough to be happy and sleep well.

Sometimes he dreamed that the force field had broken, and then all the German and Japanese and Italian war machines came screaming into the lovely city of London, burning everything and leaving nothing but a great black pit in the earth. Sometimes he dreamed that he was walking, walking, walking—until he fell off the edge of the world, tumbling round and round down a great tunnel of darkness. Sometimes he dreamed that he was completely alone, that London was empty, and that he was the only person who had ever been able to bleed.

The odd child, the child who disappeared, came into Michael's bad dreams. And remained in his dreams for ever. Because, although the little boy disappeared after the incident at play school, Michael was determined that he should not wholly disappear. Now and then, before he drifted off to sleep, Michael deliberately recalled the terrifying scene so that the child whose name he did not know would enter his dreams and be part of him for always.

It had happened one day when the paints were being used, when large sheets of paper had been clipped to all the easels, and when Miss Nightingale had told the children how splendid it would be if they all painted pictures of their fathers and mothers.

The group of children had been painting happily and noisily and messily for a while. Then suddenly the odd child had splashed paint all over his picture, had thrown his brush on the floor and had just stood there, shaking and screaming.

Miss Nightingale had not been in the room when it

happened. But she came back very quickly and tried to comfort the little boy.

"What is it, cherub?" she asked gently. Cherub was a favourite word of Miss Nightingale's. "What has happened? Has somebody been naughty and spoiled your lovely painting?"

"I hate all the children!" sobbed the odd little boy. "I hate every boy and girl! I hate myself!"

"Why?" asked Miss Nightingale. "Why do you have this terrible hate?"

"Because we are not people," he screamed. "Because we are not real people ... Because none of us can take off our heads!"

Miss Nightingale did not try to reason with him. She did not say anything. She just picked him up very gently and carried him, still kicking and screaming, out of the room.

That was the last Michael ever saw of him.

Later, Miss Nightingale said that the little boy had been ill because he had had too many bad dreams. And she asked everyone to forget what had happened because it was much more sensible to remember good things than bad things. It was thinking about bad things that brought bad dreams and unhappiness.

After several days, hardly any of the children remembered the incident; and even if they did, they remembered different versions.

But Michael remembered. And he promised himself he would always remember. Because, somehow, he knew that it was important to remember the bad things.

Even the dreams.

THREE

Michael did not know how old he was, but he knew quite a lot about what went on in the world. He learned about what was happening from the news broadcasts on the wireless; and sometimes there were programmes on the television, too.

He knew that Britain and America and Russia were at war with Italy and Germany and Japan. He knew that the important cities on both sides were protected by force fields which the bombers and the missiles could not penetrate. He knew that out there in the unprotected parts of the world, people were being hurt and killed and armies were fighting each other. He felt very sorry for people who were not protected by force fields; but Father said that force fields were very difficult to use, and they took a lot of energy, and that was why they only covered the most important cities.

Michael felt very lucky to be living in London, protected by a force field that he could not see.

He liked the city very much. It was clean and quiet and beautiful and safe. He was old enough to explore a little by himself; but he was not yet old enough to use a bicycle. Bicycles were only for the use of older people. But one day, when Michael was bigger, he would have a bicycle of his own. Father had said so.

But perhaps the war would be over before then, and the force field would no longer be needed. And perhaps the government would allow the cars and buses and trains to come back. He looked forward to that time, and yet he was afraid of it. How could he ever hope to cross a road, with cars and buses hurtling along it, without getting hurt? And yet people and children managed to do this. He had seen them doing it on films and on television programmes.

He remembered his first visit to the cinema. It was on a Saturday evening and it was a big occasion. Mother was dressed in a lovely green gown that swept the floor. Father wore a dark suit and a top hat. Michael was bathed and powdered and dressed in his sailor suit.

It was an important occasion because, said Father, they were going to a première which would be attended by the Queen.

The bicycles had been specially polished; and when they were rolling smoothly down Buckingham Palace Road, with Michael strapped safely on his seat behind Mother, he felt that this was the first really exciting event in his life.

There were more bicycles outside the Odeon, Leicester Square, than Michael had ever seen. A large space had been staked out for Queen Victoria's hovercar. Michael and Mother and Father joined the crowds waiting for the Queen's arrival. They did not have to wait long, and when she came, everyone began to cheer and some people were waving flags, and some were singing the National Anthem.

Sir Winston Churchill was waiting to receive the Queen and to introduce her to Mr. Spencer Tracy and Master Freddie Bartholomew. Then they went inside the Odeon cinema, and everyone else followed. It took quite a long time for everyone to get inside. The foyer was jammed with people and their children. Michael saw lots of children that he did not know, but he also caught a glimpse of Horatio Nelson. He, too, was wearing a sailor suit and looking unnaturally clean. Horatio grinned and waved, then disappeared with his mother and father in the crowd.

There were pictures of famous film stars in the foyer. Michael looked at them and asked Mother to tell him their names. Some of the names were strange and some were pretty. Greta Garbo was a pretty name, but Dustin Hoffman sounded very odd. There were also pictures of Charles Chaplin and Jane Fonda, George Arliss and Brigitte Bardot, Norma Shearer and Rudolph Valentino.

Even though the film was only in black and white, the big screen made it far more exciting than colour television. Michael thought that every child in the cinema—including himself—was crying when, near the end of the film, Spencer Tracy, as Manuel the fisherman, was dying in the sea while Lionel Barrymore had to stand and watch helplessly and Freddie Bartholomew was saying goodbye to his friend for ever.

After the film, there was a news feature showing the Germans bombing sad little villages in Vietnam, and there were also some pictures of Russian scientists and spacemen helping to build the missile bases on the moon.

At the end of the show, the lights went on and Queen Victoria stood in the royal box. Then the orchestra played God Save the Queen, and everyone stood very still.

Michael was tired. Tremendously excited and tremendously tired. He almost fell asleep on the bicycle on the way home. His head ached with excitement. But later, when he was trying to sleep, his head ached for a different reason. He felt that, during the course of the evening, he had discovered something important.

But he didn't know what it was.

FOUR

It was Miss Shelley not Miss Nightingale who told the children about the Overman legend. Miss Shelley was just as pretty as Miss Nightingale, but she had yellow hair. Michael liked her because she had taught him to count to one hundred. He had asked her several times to teach him. At first she said that he was not ready to learn. Perhaps, in the end, she just got tired of saying no. Counting was quite easy when you got the hang of it. As far as Michael knew, none of the other children could count. Perhaps they had not pestered Miss Shelley long enough.

She told the children about the Overman legend towards the end of the afternoon session of play school, when they were tired out after games and needed to rest a little before being collected by their mothers.

"Once upon a time," said Miss Shelley, "there was no one at all in the wide world but Overman. And he was very bored, so he said to himself: I must make something interesting happen. So he thought very hard, and finally he decided that he would make a man. Because he thought a man would be interesting. So he worked very hard, and at last he made a man.

"And the man was very grateful for being made and for being alive. But presently, he, too, got bored. And he said to himself: I must make something interesting happen. So he thought very hard, and finally he decided that he would make a machine. So he worked very hard, and at last he made a machine.

"It was a very good machine, a very complicated machine, and the man was very proud of it.

"He said to Overman: You created me, and I, too, can create. Look, I have created a machine.

"Overman was amused. He laughed. He said: The machine is very good, but you are more complicated. You can do things the machine cannot do. So mine is the better creation.

"The man was a bit disappointed at this. And he went away, determined to do better. Then he had a very ingenious idea. He decided to build a machine that could build a machine. This was a very hard task, and it took him a very long time. But eventually he succeeded. It was a very wonderful machine, very complicated indeed. The man was extremely proud of it.

"He said to Overman: You created me, but I think I have done something better. Look, I have created a machine that can build another machine.

"Again Overman was amused. He laughed. And then suddenly he created a woman. Then he said: See, I have created a woman. With the woman, you will be able to make children. And they in turn will grow up into men and women and make more children. So mine is still the greater creation.

"We shall see, said the man. My machine will build

more machines which will build yet more machines. We shall see whose is the greater creation.

"Then Overman laughed once more. He said: Farewell, my son in whom I am well pleased. You have amused me greatly. And now I will leave you to discover the end of the joke.

"What are you talking about? asked the man, perplexed.

"You challenged my powers, my son, said Overman, and that is good. But you have created more than you think. You have created a problem. And the problem is this: Shall men control machines, or shall machines control men?

"Then Overman yawned. He said: I am tired. I think I shall go to sleep for ten thousand years. But, if either men or machines discover the answer to the problem, wake me."

Miss Shelley looked at the circle of children. Some were gazing at her intently, some were whispering and giggling among themselves, some were fidgeting, and one or two were dozing.

Michael had listened to the story, enthralled. He said: "Is it true, Miss Shelley, the story of Overman?"

Miss Shelley smiled. "It is just a story, Michael, a legend. But perhaps there is a little bit of truth in it somewhere."

"Is Overman God?" said Horatio Nelson suddenly.

Michael looked at him with respect. It was a good question.

"I don't think so," said Miss Shelley. "Now, don't worry about the story, children. I told it just to pass the time. Now that we have all rested, I think the mothers will be arriving to take their children home."

That evening, Michael was unusually quiet. He was thinking. He was thinking about the story. Somehow, he knew that it was important.

After he had drunk his hot milk, and just before he was tucked up for sleep, Father came into his bedroom and said: "What did you think of the Overman legend, Michael?"

Michael felt very sleepy. "It was interesting," he said, "but it was just a story. And, anyway, it didn't have a proper end."

But when Father had gone, Michael suddenly became very wide awake. He had said nothing at all about the Overman legend. So how could Father know Miss Shelley had told it that afternoon?

FIVE

The children had been allowed to go off by themselves on an adventure walk in Hyde Park. They were to collect leaves. When the bell rang, they were to return to play school and there would be a prize for whoever had collected the largest number of different leaves.

The children set off in groups, but when they were a little distance from school, Michael left his group, wanting to be by himself. He wandered casually away, head down, as if he were already intent on looking for leaves.

He noticed that a girl had also left the group. She was following him. She had yellow hair, and her name was Ellen Terry.

Michael quickened his pace, but the distance between him and Ellen remained the same. Finally, he began to run.

He ran as fast as he could, without looking back. He ran until he was exhausted. Then he flung himself down on the grass, sobbing for breath, while the sweat trickled down his forehead and into his eyes.

When he had recovered himself, he sat up and gazed back. The school was out of sight. But there was Ellen Terry, not very far away, apparently looking for leaves.

Michael was still trembling a little and breathing heavily from his exertions. But Ellen looked quite at ease—not at all like a child who had run a long way at high speed.

Michael stood up unsteadily and walked back towards her. She affected not to notice, or not to be interested.

"Why are you following me?"

"I'm not following you. I am looking for leaves. Have you found any interesting ones?"

He ignored the question. "I ran away as fast as I could. I ran until I couldn't run any more. You must have run very fast to keep up with me."

"I like running," said Ellen. "It's nice."

"I want to be alone."

"You are alone."

"No I'm not. You followed me."

"I didn't follow you. I was just running. And, anyway, you are alone if you want to be alone."

"Ellen, go away. Go and look somewhere else."

"I shall go where I please."

"Or stay here, and I will go away."

"I shall go where I please."

She seemed to be laughing at him. She seemed to be deliberately tormenting him. Michael had been shaking with exertion; but now the tiredness had mysteriously gone and he was just shaking with rage.

"If you don't go away," he said, amazed at his own ferocity, "I'll kill you."

She began to laugh. With a cry of rage, he rushed at her and they both fell on the ground. Michael's fingers were round her neck tight. But she didn't seem to mind.

She was still laughing. He lifted her head and banged it hard on the ground, again and again. But still she laughed as if it was all no more than a game. In desperation and humiliation, he tried to bite her throat. He bit until the teeth ached in his jaw, but still the laughter came.

Suddenly, his rage and energy were spent. He let Ellen go and lay there with his face hidden by his arm, crying with misery and sheer humiliation.

The laughter stopped. Presently he felt Ellen touch him gently. She began to stroke his hair.

He sat up and looked at her, wiping the tear stains from his face and trying to understand what could not be understood.

Ellen's hair was untidy and there were bits of grass and smears of soil on her dress. But she seemed unhurt. She seemed amazingly unhurt.

"Poor Michael," she said softly. "I was only teasing. I teased you too much. Poor Michael."

"I—I tried to kill you," he sobbed, wondering at the blind fury that had possessed him.

"No, you didn't," she said positively. "You tried to hurt me, that is all."

"I didn't hurt you?"

She shook her hair and laughed. "I'm very strong ... Do you still want me to go away?"

"Yes. I'm unhappy. I want to be by myself."

"Then I'll go. Don't forget to come back to school when the bell rings ... I'm sorry, Michael. I won't tease you any more."

She stood up, smiled at him once again, then began to run away. She ran lightly, effortlessly. She ran as if she could go on like that for ever.

Presently, Michael picked himself up and began to wander about aimlessly, looking for leaves. He found several, the usual ones—oak, sycamore, willow, chestnut, beech—the ones everyone else would take back. He tried to forget about Ellen and concentrate on leaves. He wanted a leaf that no one else would have.

"Michael Faraday can't fight girls!" The words seemed to come from nowhere.

Michael spun round, but there was no one to be seen. Then he looked up. Horatio Nelson was sitting on the lowest branch of a large oak. He grinned at Michael and slithered back along the branch, climbing carefully down to the ground.

"Fight me," said Horatio.

"I can't. You know that."

"That's right ... I can beat anybody—anybody except them."

"Except who?"

"Except them. The others. *You* know."

"Yes, I know," said Michael gloomily. "Horatio, why are we afraid to talk about it?"

"To talk about what?"

"The—difference."

"I'm not afraid to talk about it."

"Would you talk about it to them?"

"No."

"Would you talk about it to your mother and father?"

Horatio pulled a face, made a noise signifying disgust. "I tried. They said I wasn't old enough to understand. They said I must not get worried about silly ideas."

"Would you talk about it to Miss Nightingale?"

"No."

"But you will talk about it to me?"

"You are like me," said Horatio, "not like them ... Children like us, we have to—to ..." he floundered.

"To trust each other?" suggested Michael.

29

"Something like that ... I saw you at the cinema last Saturday."

"I saw you, too." Then Michael suddenly remembered something that had seemed very important. "Did you see Freddie Bartholomew talking to the Queen?"

"Yes."

"He's bigger than us," said Michael excitedly. "He's much bigger. Do you think he bleeds?"

Horatio was silent for a moment or two. Then he said: "Can't tell. Not unless he was hurt ... Some of *them* are bigger than us."

"Some of them are smaller, too," pointed out Michael. "But we are all about the same size."

They heard the bell ringing in the distance.

Horatio sighed. "We'd better go back, or they'll ask questions. Give me some of your leaves. I haven't got any."

"The important thing," said Michael with a flash of insight, "is for us to go on trusting each other and for us to go on trying to find things out, until we are old enough to understand."

"Be careful," advised Horatio. "Be very careful. They don't like us trying to find things out." Then he added calmly: "If you really want to kill Ellen Terry, you will have to push her out of a high window."

Michael looked at him in astonishment. There was a question he was too afraid to ask.

SIX

Michael had a bad dream. He was with a number of other children, including Horatio Nelson, Ernest Rutherford, Jane Austen and Emily Brontë—all children who could bleed. Each child stood naked, feet buried in soft earth in a plant pot. The room was big, like a greenhouse; and the sun was shining through great, misted panes of glass.

The children stood motionless amid shrubs and tall, potted flowers. Every now and then, the gardener came with a huge watering can. He watered the flowers, the shrubs and the children. Michael wanted to talk to him; but he could not open his mouth. He could not move at all. The gardener had the face of Michael's father.

When the gardener watered the children, the water turned into blood and dripped in terrifying, criss-crossing streams down their small pale bodies. Emily Brontë seemed to be weeping tears of blood. Horatio Nelson had a fixed grin on his face, and the red stream dripped from the corners of his mouth.

Michael strained and strained to open his lips. Finally, with a great effort, he was able to speak.

He said to the gardener: "Why do you treat us like—like plants?"

The gardener laughed. "Because you are not real people," he said in a voice that echoed through the greenhouse. "You can't be made. You have to be grown. You are weak. If I don't look after you very carefuly, you will all shrivel up and die."

"Do real people bleed?" asked Michael.

The gardener was amused. "*Real* people don't need to bleed," he thundered. "*Real* people are made not to bleed."

The greenhouse became a doll factory; and all the children, their feet still embedded in earth in the plant pots, watched the dolls being made.

There were big baskets of arms and legs and heads and bodies. People in overalls were fitting the parts together. But when the dolls were assembled, they were no longer dolls. They were children. They ran about, they laughed, they jumped, they talked.

One of them was Ellen Terry.

She came to Michael's plant pot. She ran round and round it until he became dizzy, just watching her. Then she stood in front of him, laughing.

"You are not a real person," she said. "Michael Faraday is not a real person. I am a real person. Look at all that blood! Horrible! Horrible!"

Michael was enraged, humiliated, afraid. Fear and anger gave him strength. Suddenly, he stepped from the plant pot and seized Ellen. He tore off her arms and threw them into a basket. Then he tore off her legs and threw them into another basket.

No one seemed to notice. The people in overalls were

still making dolls that suddenly became children.

Ellen, armless and legless, lay on the floor, looking at him, still laughing. In a burst of fury, he tore off her head and threw it into the nearest head basket. Then he kicked her body away. No one seemed to notice.

He turned to all the children still standing stiffly in their plant pots. The red blood stains made grotesque patterns all over their bodies.

Michael went to Emily Brontë. She stopped weeping and began to smile at him. He put his arms round her and tried to lift her out of the plant pot.

Then he became aware of a great deal of shouting. He whirled round and saw that all the people in overalls were running towards him. They were carrying knives and needles and scissors. The gardener was running towards him also. The gardener was brandishing a huge pair of shears.

Michael woke up screaming.

Mother came rushing into his room. She held him in her arms and let him sob against her body until he realized that he was not in a greenhouse or a doll factory but safe in bed in his own room, with the clockwork train set on the table in the corner and the toy soldiers set out in neat ranks on a chest of drawers.

Mother was talking. Her voice sounded soothing, but Michael could not concentrate on the words.

Then Father came. Michael could not look at his face. Father said how silly it was to have bad dreams, and he asked what it was all about. But Michael would not tell him.

After a time, Mother brought something warm and sweet to drink. Michael drank it quickly, and yawned and felt very tired indeed. Then he lay back and closed his eyes. There were no dreams this time. Only darkness.

SEVEN

It was Saturday afternoon, a sunny, breezy Saturday afternoon, and Michael was in St. James's Park with his kite. He was pleased at being allowed to go out alone. Mother and Father let him go out by himself quite a lot these days. He was growing bigger, older. Perhaps even wiser.

There were not many people in St. James's Park. Here and there one or two ladies in long, rustling skirts and with parasols strolled and talked with men wearing bright blazers and boaters. Here and there a few children played with hoops or bats and balls.

It was all very pretty, thought Michael. It was all extremely pretty. Just like a picture. Or a scene. A scene from a film.

He dropped his kite on the grass and, despite the sunshine, felt suddenly cold. A scene from a film! It *was* like a scene from a film. It was, somehow, too perfect, too neat. It didn't seem real.

His childish mind was incapable of grappling with paradoxes. It was real and it had to be real and yet it didn't seem real. And the people didn't seem real, and the vistas of London didn't seem real and, for all Michael knew, the entire world might not be real.

He was sweating, he was shaking, and the sweat was cold on his forehead and body. And he felt dreadfully afraid.

Then suddenly the horrible sensation left him, because he caught sight of Emily Brontë. She was sitting on a grassy bank making a daisy chain. Emily, with her dark brown hair and wide blue eyes was real. In fact, there could be nothing more splendidly real than Emily Brontë sitting in the sunlight, making a daisy chain.

Michael picked up his kite and went to sit beside her. "Hello."

"Hello, Michael. What a marvellous kite! Will it fly?"

"Yes. I'll show you in a little while. Father made it ... Does your father make things?"

"Mother makes dolls' clothes. Father once made the dolls' house. I don't think I like dolls very much now."

Michael was silent for a while. Then he said awkwardly: "Emily, does everything seem all right to you?"

"How do you mean?"

He gestured with his arm. "All this—the park, the people ... The way we live." He floundered.

Emily put the daisy chain down and looked at him. "I don't know what you mean ... It is real, isn't it? I mean we are real, and living is real ... I don't know what you mean."

"What about the difference?" he said with sudden force. "What about the difference between us and them?"

"Mother and Father say we are not old enough to understand," said Emily calmly. "They say that when

35

we are old enough we will be able to understand everything."

"I bet most of these people are *them*," said Michael. "I bet most of the people in London are *them*! *We*—we are the strange ones. They know they are all right. I don't know that I'm all right ... I'm sorry, Emily. I don't know how to say what I want to say."

She put a hand on his shoulder. "Don't worry, Michael. Don't be upset. One day we shall understand. I'm sure of it."

Michael liked the touch of her hand. He was sorry when she took it away and let it rest lightly on the grass. He wondered what would happen if he touched it with his own hand. He decided to find out. Nothing happened. Emily did not take her hand away. He held it, but she only smiled. He liked holding it. Emily's hand felt cool and soft. Not hard, like Ellen Terry's hand.

"I love you," he said impulsively. "I love you, Emily Brontë."

She laughed. "You are a nice boy. I love you, too."

"I always will," said Michael, not daring to look at her. "I always will love you ... There—there isn't anyone else to love."

"Don't you love your mother and father?"

"No."

Emily was silent for a while. Then she said: "I don't think I love mine, either. I like them, but I don't love them. It's funny, isn't it?"

Michael was embarrassed, and let go of her hand. "Do you know about reading?"

"No. Do you?"

"I keep asking them to let me learn," he exploded, "but they say it's not necessary. They say it's something I should do when I'm older. They say I can find out everything I need to know just by asking. But I can't. I want to read now. I want to find books and see what the words mean ... You've seen books in films, haven't you? Whole rows of them. I want rows and rows of books—not picture books. Books with words."

"I expect it won't be long before they let you learn," said Emily, soothing him. "I think I would like to be able to read, too. But I can wait." She smiled. "If nobody teaches us, I expect we can teach ourselves when we are old enough to understand."

"When we are old enough to understand!" he echoed bitterly. "That is what they always say—when we are old enough to understand. I want to understand now. Now, while—while I'm hungry."

There was a sound as of distant thunder. Then more rumbling. Then a muted banging.

Emily looked up at the sky and clapped her hands.

"Oh, look, Michael—an air raid!"

"I have just thought of something," said Michael, almost to himself. "Air raids seem to happen most of all on Saturdays. That's strange. That's very strange."

"Do you think we should go home?" asked Emily.

"Why should we? The force field protects us ... Look at that Zeppelin! You'd think the ground-to-air missiles would blow it to pieces. Perhaps that is big enough to have a force field, too."

High in the sky, the Zeppelin passed slowly over London. Streaks of tracer fire homed on it, but evidently it came to no harm. Fighter planes, German and British, appeared; and the dog fights began. A German triplane turned crazily in a tight circle until it was on the tail of a British biplane. The biplane exploded, brief and lovely as a firework. A Spitfire and a Messerschmidt collided, then spiralled downwards like broken birds, leaving black tracks down the sky. Jet fighters of both sides screamed in towards each other, writing a ragged white tracery all over the sky. The Zeppelin continued on its majestic way as if it had a charmed life.

Michael watched, fascinated. So did Emily. So did everyone else in the park, and probably everyone else in London.

Michael watched, fascinated, and thought that this, too, was like a scene from a film.

No wrecked planes would come hurtling down into St. James's Park. Michael's father had told him why. The force field protected the entire city. It was impenetrable.

And yet the crippled planes seemed to be falling. They *seemed* to be falling right down on London. But they couldn't. Because the force field covered London.

Michael tried to think of it as an invisible, upside down goldfish bowl. He tried to imagine the smashed planes and all the other debris sliding off its glass-like surface. Perhaps London was surrounded by great piles of wrecked planes and rockets.

He didn't know why, but the whole idea seemed wrong. And the planes looked as if they were falling, falling.

There were more explosions, more destruction. Then the air battle was over just as abruptly as it had started, and the sky was clear and clean once more, and the vapour trails were dying.

Yes, it was just like a scene from a film. Michael forgot how pleasant and wonderful it was to hold Emily's hand. Once again there was a cold sweat on his forehead. Once again he was shaking.

EIGHT

A frosty evening in autumn. The western edge of the sky still had a few fading streaks of crimson mingling with turquoise; but high above stars pricked the blackness like cold rapiers of fire.

Michael was walking in the Mall. He should have been home long before sunset, and Father would certainly be very severe when he did get back. But Michael loved the darkness of London, the lamps, the stillness, the empty streets.

He was not alone in the Mall. Two other people were taking a short stroll close to Buckingham Palace.

They walked towards Michael. He walked towards them. He recognised them as they walked through a circle of lamplight on the pavement. He was too surprised to be afraid.

"Boy," said Sir Winston jovially, "you should be home in bed. All children should be home in bed. Your good father will have something to say upon the matter, I do not doubt."

"Yes, sir," said Michael. "I'm sorry, sir. I'm on my way home, now."

Queen Victoria wore the big black dress like she always did, and there was a shawl round her shoulders, and the crown was on her head. She gazed down at Michael.

"Sir Winston, present the child."

"My pleasure, Ma'am." Then, to Michael: "What is your name, boy?"

"Michael Faraday."

"Your Majesty," said Sir Winston, "I have the honour to present one of your Majesty's youngest subjects, Michael Faraday."

"Good evening, your Majesty," said Michael, trying to bow. "I am very sorry if I am being a nuisance."

Queen Victoria laughed. "The child thinks he is being a nuisance, Sir Winston."

Sir Winston laughed. "Any healthy boy is a nuisance, Ma'am. That is what boys are for. Then they grow up and become bigger nuisances. Eh, Michael?"

"Yes, sir. I expect so, sir."

"Child," said the Queen, "what do you want to do when you grow up?"

"I want to understand," said Michael, almost without thinking.

"You want to understand?"

"Yes, your Majesty."

"What do you want to understand?"

"Everything," said Michael desperately. "I want to understand about people. I want to understand about machines ... I—I want to know everything there is to know."

The Queen patted his head. "You want too much, child.

40

You want far too much."

Sir Winston rumbled with laughter. "Don't you want to be a sailor, boy?"

"No, sir."

"Or an airman?"

"No, sir."

"Or an astronaut?"

"No, sir ... I just want to understand."

"Don't you want to fight the Germans, to shoot down Zeppelins, programme rockets?"

"No, sir. I want to find things out."

"An odd child," mused Queen Victoria. "But then all children are odd, are they not, Sir Winston?"

"Indeed, Ma'am. Indeed they are."

The Queen said: "I recollect now, Sir Winston, that I wish you to convey our congratulations to Generals Gordon, Kitchener and Montgomery ... They, too, were once children, no doubt." She turned to Michael. "Go home, now, Michael Faraday. Go home quickly to bed. Present your apologies to your parents and inform them that you were delayed by Queen Victoria."

"Yes, your Majesty. Thank you."

Sir Winston snapped: "Are we going to win the war, boy?"

"I don't know, sir. I expect so."

Sir Winston was amused. "He expects so! He expects so! Be off with you, boy. Hurry! Hurry! The Queen commands it."

Michael broke into a run. He ran along the Mall, listening to his feet hitting the frosty pavement. After a time he paused and looked back. But Queen Victoria and Sir Winston were nowhere to be seen.

He looked up at the stars; and oddly, for a moment, they seemed like the only real things in the entire universe.

NINE

Time passed. The war continued. Newscasts told how the conflict had spread to North Africa, India, China. Time passed. London remained impregnable. The seasons came and went. Play school ended. High school began. Time passed. Michael Faraday became tall. His voice wavered uncertainly, then the childish tones were gone for ever. Emily Brontë's lips became full, magnetic. Her body developed interesting curves. Time passed.

And the sense of oddness grew.

When he was small, Michael had felt miserably alone, believing himself to be the only one who *knew* that something was wrong, that the world was somehow concealing another kind of reality. There had even been times when, in desperation, he had tried to believe that he was mad or, at least, that his mind did not work properly and that all was well in an entirely normal world. But he could not retain belief in the notion that the wrongness lay with him. Because, for no explicable reason and without any evidence to justify his attitude, he *knew* somehow that the apparently real world was only a projection of reality, concealing, perhaps, a reality that he was not yet clever enough to discover or not strong enough to face.

But as the children grew older—the children who could bleed—Michael discovered that he was not the only one to doubt the normality of life, the reasonableness of existence. Ernest Rutherford, a thin, rather frail boy, became Michael's closest friend. Ernest had an original mind, a great imagination. He could formulate possibilities and questions that seemed obvious when he talked about them; and Michael was continually amazed that he himself had not thought of such things independently.

It was Ernest who invented the generic term for all those children and adults who did not bleed. He called them drybones. It was Ernest also who defined the ones who did bleed as fragiles—because, he said, they could easily be broken. It was Ernest who wondered why all the known fragiles were roughly the same size and probably the same age (the drybones were very evasive about time) and why no one had ever met any very small ones or any very large ones. It was Ernest who first wondered why there was never more than one fragile in any family, who estimated that the proportion of drybones to fragiles was at least ten to one, and who even speculated that London itself might be a world of its own.

It was Ernest who gave Michael confidence in himself and in his reactions, who opened the doors in his mind and drew out of Michael's personality qualities of intelligence and leadership that, in the end, amazed everyone.

They visited each other's homes and spent a great deal of time in each other's company. They conducted a systematic campaign at high school for the privilege of learning how to read. Strangely, few of the other fragiles were very interested in learning how to read. Why should they be? There were films, radio and television. There were teachers and parents to answer questions, explain things. And, in the beginning, there were very few books. Which, to Michael and Ernest, made the need for reading seem more urgent. None of the drybones were interested in reading—and this made Michael want it all the more.

High school was a spacious building in King Charles the Third Street, just off the Strand. It housed ten teachers and just over a hundred pupils. The children learned how to paint, sculpt, design and make clothes; how to cook; how to sing, dance, act; how to play football, hockey, tennis, cricket; how to make toys, furniture, ornaments; how to weave; how to make polite conversation with persons of the opposite sex; how to accept the authority and wisdom of adults at all times.

There were no lessons in history, geography, science, mathematics. But sometimes, if one persisted, the teachers would give answers to questions—evasive answers, usually, that prompted more questions. It was easy for the teachers to discourage questions. The fragiles were sensitive: the drybones seemed to have a talent for ridicule. Stupid questions deserved stupid answers.

Michael got used to being an object of ridicule. The laughter did not hurt him. Not unless Emily Brontë laughed with the rest; and that was very rare.

Mr. Shakespeare was the head teacher. He looked very old. He had white hair. Even Ernest could not decide whether he was a fragile or a drybone. He looked, somehow, like an old fragile; but he behaved more like a drybone.

Michael and Ernest were amazed when they finally persuaded Mr. Shakespeare to let them learn how to read. Michael was now nearly as tall as Mr. Shakespeare. He was so excited when Mr. Shakespeare at last agreed to explain about the alphabet and show how letters could be put together to record words that he was tempted to pick the old man up and hug him.

Mr. Shakespeare started the reading programme personally. Michael and Ernest were his only pupils. Michael and Ernest were the only fragiles for whom the prospect of reading had become obsessional. When he had identified the letters for them—ay, bee, see, dee, ee, eff, jee—and had given a few simple examples of word construction, Mr. Shakspeare gave each of them an illustrated reader and told them to go away and learn to read. Each was to report back to him when he could read the entire book.

Almost trembling with excitement, Michael and Ernest went away to begin their monumental task. It was left to them to discover that in certain situations one letter could symbolise different sounds and that in some positions some letters symbolised no sound at all, and that combinations of vowels and consonants produced sounds that could already be symbolised by other letters.

It was hard work, it was confusing, at times it was unreasonable. Michael and Ernest soon abandoned the search for a logical system in the construction and representation of words. But they persevered, discovering fragments of a system and learning to make use of those fragments.

The boys were allowed to take their first reading books home. Father thought that Michael's time could be better spent. Mother was concerned that he should not work too hard. Neither offered to help him.

After tea one day, Michael took his first reading book into St. James's Park. He and Emily often met in St. James's Park—chiefly by 'accident'. They liked to be together. He had not said anything about loving her for a long time—not, perhaps, since that day ages ago when he had held her hand and they had watched the air raid, and Michael had forgotten to fly his kite.

It was a hot summer evening, with the sun still quite high in the sky. Not many people were in the park, but Emily was already there. She was sitting on the grass where they usually sat—the spot from where they had seen the Zeppelin fly over London.

Emily was wearing a simple blue dress that buttoned all the way down the front. Recently, Michael had begun to pay considerable attention to the dresses that Emily wore. He thought she looked very pretty.

"Hello, Emily."

"Hello, Michael. You have a—a book!"

"My first reading book," he said proudly. "Would you like to hear me read?"

"You can read already?"

"Some words," he said. "Only little ones. But it won't be long before I get on to the big ones."

"I'm so happy for you," said Emily. "You wanted to read as far back as I can remember ... Read me the words you know. Point to them so that I can see."

Michael sat by her side and opened his book. "The cat sits on the mat." He read slowly but did not stumble. "The cat is fat. He has a red hat. His fur is black. He likes the mat."

"Wonderful! Wonderful!" Emily clapped her hands. "When you can really read—when you can read everything, Michael—will you teach me?"

He was surprised. "I didn't know you wanted to read so much. Why didn't you make a fuss about it at school, like Ernest and I did?"

"I was afraid," said Emily. "I was afraid of the laughter. You and Ernest didn't seem to mind."

"Ernest and I are clowns," said Michael bitterly. "We

46

don't mind being laughed at ... I wouldn't want you to laugh at me, though."

"I won't ever laugh at you," she said with intensity. "I promise."

Then she lay back on the grass and flung her arms out, gazing at the sky. The sudden movement tore one of the buttons off her dress. Michael glimpsed an entrancing swell of smooth white flesh. A tightness came into his throat. He suddenly wanted to touch Emily. He wanted to touch her, to caress her, very badly.

"Why are people so strange?" said Emily. "Why do they want us to do some things and not do others? Why is there the difference—the difference that nobody wants to talk about?"

Michael hardly heard her. He could bear it no longer. He slipped a hand in the gap in Emily's dress and let his fingers rest lightly on that deliciously soft flesh.

Emily stiffened and drew in her breath sharply. Then slowly she relaxed.

"I'm sorry, Emily," he babbled. "I didn't mean to do that. Shall I take it away? Shall I take my hand away? I wanted to touch you so much. It feels. It feels ..." He didn't know how to say how it felt because he was proud, ashamed, confused, excited and utterly surprised.

Emily remained silent for a moment or two. Michael dared to let his fingers press more heavily.

"I like your hand," said Emily. Her voice sounded suddenly different. Quite different. "I like it there ... It's—it's exciting and very close ... Should we do this?"

"I don't know. I want to do it. I want to hold tight. I want to leave my hand there for ever."

He held her breast, let his fingers play with the hard small nipple. Emily shivered and began to breathe more heavily.

47

"Michael," she murmured, "Michael, read to me. Read to me again. I want something to think about. I can't think! I can't think!"

Michael did not take his hand away. He looked at the book and said unsteadily: "The cat sits on the mat. The cat is fat. He has a red hat. His fur is black. He likes the mat."

Then he let the book go and turned to Emily, lying as close to her as he could, feeling the softness of her body, still holding her breast, looking at her face which had become the face of a stranger.

And then he kissed her, and it tasted sweet. And it didn't matter that strange and terrible fevers were racking his body. And reading was forgotten, and drybones didn't matter any more, and London itself was a world that was very far away.

TEN

Michael and Ernest and Horatio and Emily and Jane formed the habit of meeting in the Coffee House in the Strand on Saturday mornings. They were friends, they trusted each other. They had a private joke. They called themselves the Family.

Several other fragiles used the Coffee House besides the Family. There were, for example, Charles Darwin and Dorothy Wordsworth—who seemed to have formed a neat little family of two—Joseph Lister, James Watt and Mary Kingsley. But while the Family liked these fragiles and remained friendly with them, it never entirely trusted them.

The Family, as Ernest frequently reminded everyone, was something special. It was composed of people (Ernest affected a note of cynicism when he used the word people) who trusted each other entirely and would not knowingly betray any secrets.

Many drybones also frequented the Coffee House. For

his own amusement, Horatio Nelson publicly affected to be a great liker of drybones—or not to notice the difference. He liked to cultivate the girls. Sometimes he would get them to go walking in the park with him; and then he would fondle them and kiss them. And he assured the Family that none of them had ever displayed any adverse reaction or showed any sign of pain when he bit their lips or pinched their breasts.

The drybones who came to the Coffee House were mostly people from high school or known adults. But occasionally there were one or two strangers.

One such stranger attempted to gain the confidence of the Family. He was the first drybone who genuinely seemed to want to communicate. Because of that, Michael was doubly suspicious.

The drybone had yellow hair and he was taller than any of the boys in the Family. He took his cup of coffee and came to their table.

"Do you mind if I sit here?" he asked with a smile.

"It's a free country," said Horatio coldly.

"At least," amended Ernest, "so we have been told."

Michael was sitting next to Emily. The drybone sat on the bench on her other side. Instantly, Michael hated him.

"My name is Aldous Huxley. I'm from North London high school."

The Family looked at each other in surprise.

"We didn't know there was a North London high school," said Jane. "We—we thought ours was the only school in London."

"Ah," said Aldous Huxley, looking round as if to make sure he would not be overheard, "until recently we were in the same position. We did not know about Central London high school."

Ernest studied him intently. "Do you have any people

like us?" he asked, placing a slight emphasis on 'us'.

"Yes." Aldous Huxley leaned forward and spoke softly. "Have you noticed that nobody ever wants to talk about— about the difference? They treat us like children. I don't want to be treated like a child. I want to know what it is all about. Don't you want to know what it is all about?" He gazed at each of them in turn.

Michael and Ernest looked at each other. Suddenly, Michael sensed danger. "We are not worried," he said easily. "We have good teachers. They will explain all we need to know when we are ready to understand."

"But don't you ever feel that there must be some kind of conspiracy?" said Aldous. "Don't you feel that infor- mation is being deliberately kept from you—by your parents, as well?"

"But that's exactly—" began Emily. Michael stopped her, pressing his leg hard against hers.

"—What we don't feel," he went on quickly. "There are lots of things that puzzle us. There are things we simply can't understand. But we have confidence in our parents. If there are things they don't want to tell us yet, there must be good reasons."

Horatio gazed at him in astonishment, but Ernest picked up Michael's line of thought without any hesitation. "We are not dissatisfied or unhappy," he said. "We enjoy life. Do you people in North London have problems?"

Oddly, Aldous Huxley seemed puzzled for a moment or two, as if the conversation was developing in a way he had not expected. Then he recovered himself. "Take the ques- tion of reading. We find that *they* try to discourage us. Doesn't that seem peculiar?"

"Not really," parried Ernest. "Reading is not all that important. We can get all the information we really need from teachers, parents, television, radio, films ... Do you know what I think? I think you people in North London must worry too much. The main thing is to enjoy life."

"What about the difference, then? Why don't they explain clearly about the difference?"

"There are two possibilities," said Michael. "One is that it is not important and the other is that it may be too difficult for us to understand yet ... I'm sorry, but my friends and I have to go now. It has been an interesting talk."

"Why don't we meet again—say next Saturday?" suggested Aldous. "I could bring some friends."

"That would be splendid, but most of us are rather busy these days. Nice to have met you."

They left Aldous Huxley drinking his coffee, and looking oddly as if he did not know what to do.

When they were outside the Coffee House, Emily said: "I can't understand what's happening. That is the first one who has really tried to talk to us, and you—"

"Not now," said Michael softly. "Not now. Let's go to Green Park. We'll talk there."

It was a warm bright morning, but there were not many people in Green Park. The Family found a patch of grass that was secluded enough for their purposes and sat down. They looked expectantly at Michael.

"Now listen to what I am going to say," he began, "and then you can tell me I'm crazy. Emily was quite right. Aldous Huxley is the first one who tried to talk to us, and that is why I was afraid. He said he came from North London high school, of which we have never heard. It probably exists. If so, we'll find it. But there is one absolutely basic principle for the survival of the Family. We must not let any drybone, however interesting he seems, get any useful information from us at all."

"Hear, hear," said Ernest. "Michael is dead right. We

are children, we are babes in arms. They have all the power."

"A drybone is a drybone is a drybone," added Horatio with a grin. He turned to Jane. "If I bit your lip, Jane, you'd cry. If I pinched your breast, you'd scream. If I hit you, you'd fall down. Not them. As we all know, they go on for ever."

Emily said helplessly. "We can't stay in isolation. We can't spend our lives like this."

"We can, we must, we will," retorted Michael fiercely. "Or until we know exactly what it is all about. We five are close. In a way we love each other. I suppose that is why we think of ourselves as the Family. But we are more than a family. We have to be. We are a sort of fighting unit —not in the sense of making war, but in the sense of being determined to discover the truth. The truth may be crazy—or it may drive us crazy. But we have to find the kind of truth that satisfies us, not the kind that could so easily be supplied by them. We cannot let them find out what we are really like until we have found out what they are really like. We can accept no risks. Anything from a drybone at all, any act of friendship, should be suspect."

"Do you hate them?" asked Jane. "Or are you afraid?"

"Afraid," confessed Michael, "not so much of what they will do to us as of what we may be to them."

Ernest gave a twisted smile. "We may be their pets— like rabbits. Or they might be part of some elaborate system designed by someone or something simply to look after us. I don't believe anything I'm told, any more—the war, the outside world, anything. I don't disbelieve it either. But I am only ever going to believe what I—or we —personally can prove."

"Ernest has hit it," said Michael. "They may treat us as children, they may conceal as much as they wish.

But we know that we are children no longer. The games, the amusements, the diversions don't satisfy us. We need something more. We need the truth. We need to stop being bewildered and absorbed in our own nightmares. We need to plan a campaign of investigation—a campaign to which we are all dedicated and which *they* do not suspect. ... I only wish we had someone to guide us."

He stopped and looked at his companions. They were all looking steadily at him.

Ernest said: "We have someone to guide us, Michael. I'm afraid that is your job ... I have some intelligence, but I am not too strong on courage, I think." He grinned. "With Horatio, it seems to be the reverse. As for Jane and Emily—well, isn't the responsibility too much? So that leaves you."

Michael looked at the Family, and said nothing. Because there was nothing to say. Somebody had to do it. Somebody had to make the mistakes and know it was his fault when things went wrong. But now, he realised, he was five times more afraid than before. And that, too, was something he would have to keep to himself.

Emily touched his hand, and was surprised to find it very cold.

ELEVEN

The Family was now psychologically committed. Until that Saturday morning in Green Park, it had been no more than a group of friends, drawn to each other by loneliness, fear, frustration, lack of hard facts and the acute awareness of their common physical difference from the drybones. But now the Family was in the process of becoming an underground movement, an escape committee dedicated to escaping from the labyrinthine ignorance in which the drybones seemed to wish to keep all fragiles.

Their overt behaviour was as it had previously been, as was expected of them. They went to high school and endured the normal routine of creative and leisure activities. They participated in normal domestic activities with their mothers and fathers. They developed hobbies, went to the cinema, met socially, watched television, played healthy games and did their best to conform as much as possible. But secretly they began to list in order of priority questions to be answered, problems to be solved, projects to be undertaken.

Michael and Ernest continued to learn to read, but they progressed far faster than they allowed Mr. Shakespeare to suspect. At the same time, and secretly, they began to teach Horatio and Jane and Emily—who, in public, still showed no interest in reading at all. From reading, the art of writing followed naturally. Michael and Ernest were soon able to copy the shapes of the letters quickly. Thus they were able to preserve and communicate their ideas and to increase their skills so that they would be ready for the time when they could get hold of *real* books containing *real* information—if, indeed, such existed.

Mr. Shakespeare restricted them to a diet of easy reading books containing only children's stories. Perhaps, thought Michael, he hoped to discourage them, to bore them, so that in the end they would think that reading had nothing to offer.

Drybone or fragile—they were still not sure which—Mr. Shakespeare was an enigmatic person. Most days he seemed to exhibit a completely drybone personality. But just occasionally, he revealed something more. While apparently discouraging them from reading, he also held out the possibility—as usual, when they were ready for it— that one day Michael and Ernest might be allowed to visit the library. He would not tell them where the library was, and Michael and Ernest searched the streets of central London in vain, but he said enough to convince them of its existence.

The Family took to meeting very regularly to consider the task it had set itself and to work out what Michael was fond of calling the strategy of investigation. Such meetings were not kept secret from fathers and mothers or other drybones. They were merely disguised as social activities of one kind or another. For all practical purposes, the Family was simply a group of adolescents indulging in the accepted rituals and sudden enthusiasms of adolescents.

The list of questions to be answered became formidable. Why did fragiles have drybone parents? Why (Mr. Shakespeare possibly excepted) were there no adult fragiles? How were fragiles made? How were drybones made? How big was London? Was it possible to leave the city? Was there really another high school containing fragiles as well as drybones? Did the library exist? Was there really a world outside London in which other, similar cities existed and in which wars were being fought? Had the Americans, if they existed, landed on Mars, if it existed? What was real and what was unreal? Who was mad and who was sane?

All tabu questions—questions that the drybones would dismiss, laugh away as absurd or counter with "You are not yet old enough or intelligent enough to understand." But, as Ernest claimed, if anyone really wanted to understand he must be intelligent enough to understand at least some of the truth.

"All our lives," said Michael, late one evening when the Family had gathered on the lamplit Embankment, "they have tried to keep us under a kind of intellectual sedation. They have done their best to educate us against initiative, against exploration. Which makes it especially difficult, because not only do we have to fight against the drybones' conspiracy, we have to fight against ourselves—against the fears they have planted, against the urge to play safe and stay secure." He looked at Emily. "We may even have to fight against personal feelings and emotions if they weaken our determination to discover what it is all about."

"Talk, talk, talk," said Horatio disgustedly. "Why don't we do something? Why don't we get something going? It

57

will make us feel a lot better."

"Providing it is not dangerous," added Jane. "I mean really dangerous."

"How do we know what is dangerous?" asked Ernest. "Speaking for myself, ignorance is dangerous to my sanity. I know that."

"Horatio is right," said Michael. "The time has come to do something. There's one thing I'm sure of—it won't be long before the drybones discover that we're not just playing at being ordinary young people any more. It will be interesting to see what they do."

"It is more interesting," observed Horatio, "to concentrate on what *we* are going to do."

Michael grinned. "Horatio, you will live to regret this zest for action—while you are counting your blisters." He turned to the rest. "First, we are going to do what we should have been able to do a long time ago. We are going to find out about London ... It has struck me as very odd that we are still not allowed to have bicycles. Why aren't we? The answer sticks out, doesn't it? They want to keep us confined to a small area of the city. In fact, when you come to think of it, all the activities they organise for us, all the excursions we are allowed to make never seem to get us very far from the centre of the city.

"We could steal bicycles, but that is asking for trouble —an open declaration of war. So we shall just have to do our exploration the hard way, on foot and as inconspicuous as possible. Next Saturday, Emily and I are going to have a picnic. Except that it won't be a picnic. We are going to walk downstream, following the Thames as far as we can before we have to turn back. The Thames is supposed to flow into the sea. Perhaps we shall reach the sea. I don't know, because we don't have any hard facts even about simple things like distances. Perhaps we shall come up against the force field or be turned back by something else. But at least we will find out something—even if it is only that we can't discover much in a day's journey."

"What about us?" asked Horatio.

"You have the harder task. I want the three of you to combine your efforts on two projects: one, you are to systematically look for a library—I assume there would be some sign to indicate such a building—and, two, you are to make a drawing of the pattern of the main streets. When you have covered central London, you spread out ... You have heard about maps, haven't you? Proportional drawings of places. I remember seeing one or two in films and on television. Well, eventually, we shall wind up with a map of London."

"If the drybones don't manage to wreck the project first," said Jane.

Ernest sighed. "I wish we had a compass. I've seen those in films, too. You know, the drybones must be stupid, otherwise they would not let us learn about things like books, maps, compasses and all the other things they don't want us to have."

Michael was silent for a moment or two. Then he said: "On the other hand, it could be that they *want* us to know about the things they won't let us have. Maybe they want us to realise how much we are being denied."

Emily shivered. "It's cold, now, and it's late. We'd better go home. There will be questions."

Horatio laughed bitterly. "There always are. Their questions, not ours. If I could kill Father and Mother and get away with it, I really would."

Nobody was surprised at the intensity in his voice. Nobody was shocked at the thought he expressed.

TWELVE

Michael and Emily did not dare to start their picnic too early. It might have aroused suspicion. Michael was pessimistically sure that their exploration projects would be discovered sooner or later—but later, he hoped, rather than sooner.

Emily lived in a small house in Victoria Street. He called for her quite late in the morning. Mr. Brontë looked younger and less severe that Michael's father. Mrs. Brontë had a slightly more attractive face than his mother, but otherwise she looked pretty much the same and dressed pretty much the same. The Garbo look had become fashionable with some of the older drybones. Mrs. Brontë had her hair done like Greta Garbo's in *Queen Christina*.

Emily wore a white dress and a wide-brimmed straw hat. She looked, thought Michael, delicious. One day he would live with Emily Brontë in a home of their own, far away from all the drybones, far away from all the nightmares, far away from London. One day ...

Mrs. Brontë had the picnic basket ready. She asked Michael where he wanted to take Emily. He said Hampstead Heath. Hampstead Heath was far enough away to make the picnic seem like a special jaunt, but not too far away to excite suspicion.

Mr. Brontë took Michael on one side and said that Emily was a fine girl and that he wouldn't want any harm to come to her, and that he was sure Michael was man enough to control himself. Michael was embarrassed and said he would never do anything to hurt or upset Emily and that he liked her very much indeed and would do his best to protect her from all harm.

It was just like in the films. Mr. Brontë seemed to want it that way.

They did not manage to get away from Emily's house much before lunch time. They were already hungry by the time they had reached the Embankment. Michael was carrying the picnic basket. He took out a couple of apples for him and Emily to eat as they walked.

They walked past Westminster Bridge, Waterloo Bridge, Blackfriars Bridge, Tower Bridge. There was a short air raid while they were between Blackfriars Bridge and Tower Bridge. No Zeppelins this time, only biplanes and triplanes. It seemed more like a kind of circus act than aerial combat. The action seemed to take place directly over the Tower of London. As usual, the wrecked planes fell into nothingness—swallowed, apparently by the invisible force field.

Michael had never before been further than the Tower of London. As they passed into unknown territory his excitement grew. Presently, they were tired and needed to rest a little. They sat on a low wall and ate some of the sandwiches and drank some milk. They were in an area of docks, of large blank buildings and cranes and quaysides. But there were no ships. Michael's father had once said that while the war was on, ships no longer unloaded in the Port of London. Michael had wondered why. Perhaps it was not possible to lift the force field to let the ships through. But, in that case, how did supplies reach London? He sighed. Mysteries, mysteries ...

It was a grey day, but the air was warm. Michael suddenly realised that there were no people about, none at all. That was pleasant and unusual. Usually, there were at least one or two people about. Their absence gave a delicious sense of freedom. And then he realised that they had met no one since they had passed the Tower of London. Curious!

Emily, apparently, had the same thoughts. "Isn't it wonderful, being entirely alone for once. I wonder where everybody is?"

"I don't suppose we can expect people to live in this kind of area," suggested Michael. "Besides, I don't think ships come this far up the river any more. So there isn't any work to be done ... Are you very tired?"

"Not tired at all, now," said Emily bravely. "*We* have work to do, haven't we? We ought to be moving on. It won't be long before we have to turn back, otherwise we shall be very late, and there will be trouble ... We are not doing very well, so far, are we? No great revelations, no mysteries solved."

"We are new to the discovering business," said Michael lightly. "It would be unreasonable to expect too much from our first attempt. Come on, love. Let's just do the best we can."

"You called me love," said Emily. "That's nice. That's very nice."

"You are my love," said Michael, surprised at his own lack of shyness. "The cat sits on the mat—remember?"

"The cat sits on the mat," repeated Emily. She smiled. "The most beautiful words in the world ... I wish the cat would sit on the mat again, Michael."

"My love, it will. But not here, not now."

Rested a little and refreshed, they began to walk once more. There was urgency in Michael's step. He badly wanted the expedition to be worthwhile. It would be depressing if this first project revealed nothing. Every now and then, he had to consciously slow down, realising that the pace he set was too fast for Emily.

At times they had to leave the river, but always they managed to get back to it. Now they were past the docks and suddenly in open country. Nothing but grass and trees and hedges and birds. In theory the Thames should have been widening; but it did not look very wide. It looked, somehow, insignificant.

Still no people. No people. Absolutely no people. Michael began to feel excited, not knowing why. The grey sky was darkening perceptibly.

Emily said: "Michael, we ought to turn back."

He squeezed her hand. "Just a little longer. There has to be something."

Presently, Emily said firmly: "I'm sorry, dear. I need to rest. Then we must turn back. If we are too late, they may not let us go off alone any more."

"How would they stop us?" he demanded savagely. "All right, Emily. You stay here and rest. I'll go on a bit, then I'll turn back. We'll both turn back." Now he felt tired and empty and frustrated.

Emily sat down thankfully on a grassy bank. She lay back and let out a great sigh. Michael left the picnic basket with her. Then he forged ahead, almost running in his desperation to find something of value. The river swung in a broad turn. It took him a long time to get round the bend, longer than he would have thought. But what he discovered, standing on a small rise, justified all the effort.

The Thames had turned back upon itself. There, in the distance, was the city skyline. The Thames was not flowing down to the sea. It was flowing back to London.

The implications hit him with an almost physical impact. He was no longer depressed. He forgot his fatigue. Excitement tingled through his limbs. He began to laugh hysterically, and had to make an effort to stop. All he had found was another mystery, but at least he had found something.

He rushed back to Emily falling down twice in his eagerness to reach her and tell her the news. At first, she simply refused to believe it.

"But it can't, Michael. It can't ... It just can't go back to London."

"Emily, it does—and we are going on to prove it."

"Oh, Michael. It's silly, but—but I'm terribly afraid. I'm afraid that something dreadful will happen."

He lifted her up and kissed her gently without passion, almost oblivious of the soft breasts that pressed against him.

"Nothing dreadful will happen, I promise. We go on. We must go on. I promise we will not be home too late."

It was dark long before they got home. But not too dark for Michael to discover, triumphantly, the secret of the Thames. Emily was exhausted, but bravely she somehow managed to keep on going. It was dusk by the time they came to Richmond Bridge, darker by the time they passed Kew Bridge. The moon was high when they reached Chelsea Bridge. The next bridge would be Westminster. Back full circle! There was no need to follow the Thames any further. It was not a river. It was just a great, uneven ring of flowing water.

From Chelsea Bridge to the Brontë house in Victoria Street was not far; but to Emily it seemed an endless distance. Michael felt sorry for her and guilty at having made her walk so far; but the guilt was submerged in a heady sense of elation.

When they reached Victoria Street he made Emily rest a little before he took her home. They both realised it was important for her not to arrive back in a distressed condition.

Michael cooked up a cover story; and when they reached the Brontë house, Emily—with tremendous effort—walked as if she felt quite fresh and had enjoyed a pleasant picnic. Michael hobbled, wincing with pain.

He apologised to Mr. and Mrs. Brontë for not returning Emily earlier; but he had had the bad luck to sprain his ankle on Hampstead Heath, and he had needed to take several rests on the way back.

Mr. Brontë lectured him on being careless and on his duty to ensure that Emily came home at a reasonable time. He hoped that Michael would be more careful in future, otherwise it might not be possible for him to take out Emily alone. Michael assured Mr. Brontë that he really was very sorry and that he would be much more careful in future. Mrs. Brontë wanted to bathe his ankle; but Michael thanked her and assured her that he would prefer to wait till he got home.

Emily walked down the garden path with him. She kissed him very quickly and said: "I love you." Then she went back into the house and closed the door.

Michael gazed up at the stars, high over a river that was not a real river. High, perhaps, over a world that was not a real world.

He was too tired to think clearly; but he knew that something very important had been achieved.

THIRTEEN

"So we are contained," said Ernest grimly. "The Thames it not a river flowing to the sea, and what we call London is surrounded by a vast moat. There is no truth but untruth. There is no reason but unreason."

Ernest and Michael were standing on Waterloo Bridge. The afternoon session of school had ended. Shortly they would separate and go home for tea.

"All these bridges," said Michael. "The roads have to go somewhere."

"Do they?" Ernest was bitter. "I doubt it. Something tells me that our little world is full of subtle circles ... Sometimes I feel that we must be like animals in a zoo or—or tender plants that have to be raised in a greenhouse."

Suddenly, Michael remembered fragments of the dream he had had long ago—long before he had begun to shave, long before he had discovered the sweet excitement lurking in Emily's rounded body. Long ago in a world of night-mare innocence.

He told Ernest all that he could remember of the dream. Then, for a minute or two, neither of them said anything. At last, Ernest broke the silence.

"A greenhouse," he said. "A greenhouse ... Let us suppose the absurd. Let us suppose that the drybones can control our dreams in some way, perhaps even some of our waking thoughts ... Your nightmare could have been manufactured. It could have been used as—as a kind of preparation." He shrugged. "Just a crazy notion to fit a crazy situation."

"It doesn't matter that it's crazy," said Michael. Then he added strangely: "What does matter is that it is not—not elegant. I mean, it doesn't feel right. It feels ... It feels ... Oh, I don't know what I mean."

Ernest grinned. "I like your use of words. Not elegant, I must remember that. *I* know what you mean, though. You reject the idea because it is untidy. But the green-house idea—that is an elegant possibility. Outside what we call London, the climate is too cold; the winds are too fierce; the animals are too dangerous for poor creatures such as we. Right?"

"Something like that," admitted Michael. "We are prisoners, but protected prisoners."

"Perverse, protected prisoners," corrected Ernest. "We reject protection. Such is our madness that we wish to escape into danger—if danger is the price of freedom ... Or truth."

Michael stared down over the side of the bridge at the water. "How long did it take you to find the library?" he asked.

"About two hours, not more. I was too busy trying to make a map to pay much attention to time. It is in an odd little place called Apollo Twelve Square, about twenty minutes away from Piccadilly Circus. I'm sure I have seen Apollo Twelve Square before. I used to go walking by myself quite a lot before we joined the Family. But I didn't notice it."

"Perhaps because you couldn't read the words," ventured Michael.

"Perhaps. I ought to have noticed it, though. It is the most shabby building in the square. It's all boarded up, and it looks as if it has not been used for a thousand years." He laughed mirthlessly. "Why should it be used? Nobody needs to read. Nobody wants to read."

"Except us."

"Except us. And we are crazy."

Michael was still staring at the water. "In the country of the mad," he murmured, "the sane man is crazy."

"What did you say?" There was urgency in Ernest's voice.

"Oh, nothing much. I'm sorry. I was just thinking and talking to myself. I'm sorry, Ernest."

What did you say?

Michael looked at him in surprise. "In the country of the mad, the sane man is crazy ... You said that we were crazy and—"

"You've got it!" Ernest was almost dancing with excitement. "You have defined the predicament. You have stated our philosophy."

"Now, who's drunk on words? The drybones don't use words like that. You only get them from flat people on a screen. People you can't talk to. So how do you know what the words mean?"

"Because I *do* know. Because I collect words. I compare them, I define them. They are precious tools. You need words to think ... What about all the thoughts you couldn't have—until you found words to fit them?"

Michael laughed at his intensity. "All right, Ernest. Calm down. So the world is mad and we are crazy because we are sane. It gets us no further. Let us keep to the facts. You are sure the words were London Library?"

"Absolutely sure. I copied them down. I didn't know how to spell library before. But now I'll know until I die."

"And you are sure that you were followed?"

"No, I'm not. But Horatio is. I was too busy with the map. Horatio is positive we were followed. He says that one drybone stayed with us for about six streets, then another took over, and then another."

"Did Jane notice anything?"

"She thinks we might have been followed, but she is not sure. Horatio said the drybone was always about a hundred paces behind us. He made Jane take a rest and stay behind a bit until one of them passed. Then she followed the drybone. But Horatio says that when we turned into another street the drybone disappeared and another took over. Jane did not see the switch."

"Just assuming you were being followed, what made Horatio think they were drybones and not fragiles?"

Ernest smiled faintly. "As you know, drybones are Horatio's special study. I can't tell them at a distance, but Horatio seems to be able to, even when he can't see their hair. I don't know how he does it, but I have seen him identify drybones and fragiles correctly in a group quite far away."

"We had better assume the worst, then. You were followed, and at least one drybone knows that you found the library—if it is a library."

"Were you and Emily followed?"

"I don't think so. No. I'm sure we weren't. We were really alone, especially in the open country ... I wonder if the drybones thought you were being systematically curious or just idly curious."

Ernest thought for a moment or two. "They must have known that I was drawing a map."

"You could have been sketching interesting pieces of architecture."

"I don't think they would fall for that."

"I don't either. But they might. Still, if we spend our time worrying too much about what the drybones know or suspect, we'll never get anything done. We must just proceed as if all is well until somebody stops us."

"Or takes us into protective custody," added Ernest. "Just like the Gestapo."

Michael stared down at the water once more. "It isn't a river but it flows." Suddenly he laughed. "I like that. I like it very much. Splendid attention to detail ... Well, I suppose it is time we went home and behaved normally —in the faint hope that we are deceiving somebody."

"What is the next project?" asked Ernest.

"You found London Library, but we don't know if it contains any books. So, Ernest, we will just have to see."

"So soon? The drybones will expect us to go back."

"Also part of the project," said Michael grimly. "A test case, if you like. I expect the drybones will expect us to go back."

FOURTEEN

It was late evening. Mother and Father and Michael had just returned from the cinema. They had been to see *Gone With The Wind*. Mother had made hot drinks. Michael was sipping his slowly.

"You must get to bed soon, Michael," said Father. "It has been a long evening. Then you will be fresh for school tomorrow. Did you enjoy the film?"

"Yes, father. It was very good ... Was there really a war between the north and south in America?"

"I just love Vivien Leigh," said Mother. "She is such a great actress. Mind you, she had a perfect match in Clark Gable. What a handsome pair they were."

"Was there really a civil war?" persisted Michael.

Father took a drink of milk, although Michael still found his far too hot. Mother and Father never seemed to notice when food or liquids were too hot to eat or drink.

"Well, now, that is an interesting point," said Father. "Of course, you have to remember that films are only dramatic entertainment. They are concerned with emotions rather than facts. Every nation has had a civil war at some time, I suppose. Probably the Americans did."

"But you don't know."

"Son, you must realise it is not possible to keep in mind everything that has happened. The important thing is to remember important things—things that matter in your own personal life."

Michael sighed. That was the way it always went, either by a long or a short route. Suddenly he decided to try a surprise attack.

"Does the Thames flow down to the sea?"

"What a question! Michael, I think you are tired. It is time for bed. You ought to know that rivers flow to the sea."

"That wasn't what I asked. Does the Thames flow to the sea?"

"Now you are being difficult. I have just told you that rivers flow to the sea." There was a note of irritation in Father's voice. Michael recognised it. Always the same note of irritation—a few minutes before conversational cut-off, a display of anger, or a display of contempt.

But Michael went on.

"Is the Thames a river?"

"Dear boy!" The exasperation mounting. "I sometimes despair. You know what the Thames is as well as I do. Sometimes I think you try to annoy me intentionally with silly questions. Come on, it is time for bed. Let us not have a bad end to a pleasant evening." Father finished his milk and stood up.

So it always went. So it would always go. Unless somebody did something about it.

"I have another silly question," said Michael shrilly. "How was I made?"

Mother said: "Michael, it is very late. Let us go to bed, and leave these questions till tomorrow, when we are fresh."

Michael glared at her. "The standard response. Wait till tomorrow. Wait till you are old enough to understand. Wait! Wait! Wait! I have done a long stint of waiting. All my life so far. I'm half out of my mind with waiting. Perhaps that is what you want."

Father was stern. "I will not have you speaking to Mother like that. Apologise at once, boy!"

"What will you do if I don't—beat me? I'm a bit big for that, but drybones are stronger than fragiles, so I suppose you could do it."

Father seemed surprised. Oddly, there was less anger in his voice. "What is all this nonsense about drybones and fragiles?"

Michael knew he was being reckless, but he didn't care any more. The years of deceit, the years of frustration and ignorance had built up a great pressure inside him. He had to reduce the pressure somehow. He took a deep breath.

"You are a drybone, I am a fragile. Silly definitions, perhaps, but we had to find some way of describing the difference. You people have kept us in ignorance as far back as I can remember. It looks to me as if you intend to keep us ignorant and dependent for ever. But that is something I will not stand. You can do what you like, but you cannot make me accept a condition of ignorance." He paused, trying to discern some expression in their faces, but there was only a curious blankness.

"I know you drybones are superior to us fragiles," he went on desperately. "We bleed, you don't. We can be hurt easily, you can't. We get tired, you have inexhaustible

energy. We feel pain, you don't. There are so many differ-
ences. And yet you say you are my father and mother.
So I say to you: how was I made?"

Mother sighed. "Michael, you make things so difficult.
Be a good boy and wait until morning."

"How was I made? How was I made? *How was I made?*"
Michael did not know that he was shouting.

Father sat down once more. "Well, boy, it sounds as if
you are determined." The anger had drained from his
voice. "I like determination in a man. It shows he has
character ... I'll speak plainly. You think we have been
misleading you. Has it occurred to you that we may have
been shielding you, protecting you?"

"Yes, it has occurred to us that you may be protecting
us," said Michael wearily. "But if so, it is like—like mental
suffocation."

"You want to know how you were made. I'll tell you.
You were grown from a tiny speck of life—call it an
egg ... Michael, can you remember back to when you
were very small?"

"Yes, Father."

"Do you think you could have looked after yourself
then?"

"No, Father."

"That is what we are for—we drybones, as you call us.
We were *designed* to look after you, Michael. We were
designed to rear you to maturity. We, as you know, are
different. We are designed and manufactured, we are not
grown. It is not necessary for us to feel pain or bleed. It is
only necessary for you ... You know the Overman legend,
Michael. Personally, I don't believe it. But ask yourself if
any of it could be true ... Now, I have answered your
question. Let us go to bed."

"Yes, Father." Michael felt empty, exhausted. He had

made a kind of challenge, and he did not know whether it had been accepted or dismissed.

Mother smiled. "Well, the film was pleasant, anyway. Although I must say I was a bit saddened by all that destruction ... Michael, I do wish you would not see quite so much of that Ernest Rutherford. I'm not sure he is a good influence."

Michael was too tired to argue. Too tired for anything, even rational thought. He went to bed feeling that at least he had learned something. He woke up in the morning realising that he had learned nothing.

FIFTEEN

The Family set out to visit London Library on a Saturday morning. None of them had told parents where they were going; but they made no attempt to conceal their movements. Ernest's map had been copied, and Horatio suggested that each of the Family should go to the library by a different route and that if anyone was being followed, he or she should either shake off the follower or return home. But Michael overruled the idea, preferring that the Family should stay together. He had become more interested in discovering if the drybones would attempt to frustrate the investigation than in maintaining its secrecy.

However, a compromise plan was agreed. Michael and Emily, and Ernest and Jane would make their way to the library together. Horatio would follow at some distance in an attempt to find out if the group itself was being followed.

Saturday was a grey day with promise of rain. The girls carried plastic raincoats, and the boys had their water-

76

proof jackets. Jane and Emily had brought some sandwiches, and Ernest had a bag of apples. Michael had borrowed his father's electric torch; and Horatio, for reasons best known to himself, carried a short, thick iron bar.

The promise of rain was fulfilled long before they reached the library. The sky darkened, the air became humid and there were distant sounds of thunder. Presently, the thunder came nearer, lightning was visible almost overhead and the rain came down torrentially. Warm rain, whipped a little by a warm wind, penetrating the openings in raincoats and jackets, and drenching everyone.

By the time the group reached the library, they felt soaked to the skin. They sheltered in the doorway, waiting a short time for Horatio.

"Did you see anyone following?" asked Michael.

Horatio shook his head. "I thought so at first, between Trafalgar Square and Piccadilly Circus. A female drybone —if one may use the term female carelessly. She—it looked like Edith Evans, but I couldn't be sure. Anyway, she evidently wasn't following because nobody took over when she disappeared from the scene."

"Do you think anyone followed you?"

Horatio grinned. "No, I made quite sure of that."

London Library looked exactly as it had looked when Ernest discovered it—boarded up, unused. Shabby, old, unimportant. Michael's spirits sank. He began to think it was all part of a bad joke, a drybone kind of joke. He began to think that the books must have been taken away a long time ago.

"I don't suppose it would be much use ringing the bell," said Horatio. "We will have to break in."

"But we should ring the bell first," said Jane, "in case ..." she stopped.

"In case the place is crawling with people," suggested Horatio sarcastically.

"There is one way to find out," said Michael. He pressed the button. Everyone heard the electric bell clearly. Somehow, London Library sounded very empty.

The lightning had stopped, but the rain was still coming down very heavily. No one seemed to be about in Apollo Twelve Square. Indeed, to Michael it looked as if all the houses were as desolate and as deserted as London Library.

Horatio began to attack the boards across the doorway with his iron bar. They had only been nailed loosely and could be prized away quite easily. The door behind them did not have to be forced. It was not locked. Ernest turned the handle and opened it. The Family went in.

On the wall immediately inside the building were two switches, presumably electric light switches. Michael pressed them but nothing happened. The only light available was drab grey light filtered through grimy windows. But it was enough to reveal that Michael's pessimism was unjustified.

Inside, the library looked larger than it did from the outside. There were shelves round the walls. Most of the shelves were empty; but some of them supported untidy stacks of books.

Hundreds of books, perhaps thousands. All in careless heaps. Michael surveyed them open-mouthed. He felt like the prospectors he had seen in a film when they discovered a legendary gold-mine.

Wind caused the library door to slam, and everyone jumped. Horatio broke the tension with laughter. "Now you are all in my power," he cackled evilly. "Soon you will submit to the dreaded will of my vampire bride."

78

"Books," breathed Ernest. "Books, books, books!"

He went to the nearest pile and picked one up. Dust fell from its dark, hard cover. He saw some words printed in gold on its spine, and tried to read them in the almost nocturnal gloom.

"*Ut-o-pie-ay*, by Sir Tho-mas—Sir Thomas More ... Wonderful! Wonderful! I don't know what it is. I don't know what it is, but I'll find out ... It will take time, so much time, and I'll either die or go mad before I have finished. But I want to read every book that is here."

Michael picked up a book. He found the title easy to read: "*Das Kapital von Karl Marx.*" He opened it, but found the words inside incomprehensible. "This one isn't our language. It's another language—I wonder what it is."

Horatio was not greatly interested in books. He watched, feeling faintly superior as Jane and Emily went from shelf to shelf, fingering the books almost as if they might explode, sometimes bringing one to Ernest or Michael to have the title read.

Jane found a pile of several books, all of which constituted *The Decline and Fall of the Roman Empire* by Edward Gibbon. Emily came across *The Arts of Mankind* by Hendrik van Loon. Michael put *Das Kapital* down and wandered to another shelf, where he picked up *The Art of Creation* by Arthur Koestler. Ernest was trying to read some of *Utopia*, but he found it hard going and had to rest.

"I'm hungry," announced Horatio. "While you clever people are having fun, I would like to eat something."

"It is time we all ate," said Jane. "We can still look at the books while we are eating ... It really is wonderful— I mean finding the library and all these books. I do wish I could read properly. Ernest you are going to have to help me a lot."

There was a look of almost comical sadness on Ernest's face. "Help *you*!" he said wistfully. "Dear Jane, I'll have all the trouble in the world, just helping myself."

Emily shared out the sandwiches and apples. The light was getting poorer, and it was hard to read even the large print on the title pages and book covers. Michael began to use his electric torch.

"Don't flash that thing about too much," said Horatio. "It will be visible from outside. No need to advertise our presence too much to any inquisitive drybones."

"I know what I'm going to do," said Ernest excitedly. "I am going to make a little collection of books that I think I can read, then I'll take them home. When I have finished them, I can bring them back and get some more."

"Do you think that is wise?" asked Emily.

"Why not? Nobody comes here. That is obvious. Nobody wants the books, except us."

"Have you got a safe place where you can hide them?" asked Michael.

"No, but I'll find one. It won't be difficult." He munched an apple and strained to make some sense out of *Idylls of the King* by Alfred Tennyson.

Michael walked across the floor of the library, his footsteps echoing on the wooden blocks. For no apparent reason, he suddenly remembered something he had said to Ernest on Waterloo Bridge. In the country of the mad, the sane man is crazy.

He looked around the large and darkened room at the piles of dusty books that seemed as if they had been placed on the shelves in a hurry and just left there to rot. He looked at his four friends, eating sandwiches and apples, surrounded by millions of recorded words that could only be deciphered with great difficulty. He thought of the river that was not a river and of parents who were entirely different from their so-called children ... Truly, it was the country of the mad. But the important question was: who could define sanity? And if, indeed, anyone could remain sane in such an incomprehensible world, how long could they remain so?

His head ached with thinking and with trying to read. He was tired of mystery and conflict and the odd isolation of the fragiles, the loneliness that drove them to try to be brothers and sisters and teachers and even parents to each other. He was tired of being responsible for the Family. And he was tired of the fact that he would have to go on being tired for a long time.

He sighed and flashed his torch idly at a pile of books. One caught his attention. He picked it up. Slowly, laboriously he read the title. And then suddenly his tiredness was forgotten. His heart began to beat fast enough for him to be aware of the beating. He knew—he knew beyond any shadow of doubt—that the painful process of teaching himself to read would be proved worthwhile. The title of the book he held in a trembling hand was: *A Short History of the World*. The author was someone called H. G. Wells.

Michael sat down on the floor and flicked through the pages lovingly. Here and there a word caught his eye— a word that he could understand. He was oblivious of the library, oblivious of the Family. This was the book. He knew it. This was the book. *A Short History of the World!* The very words became an incantation. Now would secrets be revealed and mysteries resolved. He felt drunk. Drunk with anticipation and excitement.

Suddenly, he realised that someone was talking to him, someone was tugging his arm. It was Emily. Even in the semi-darkness he saw that there was a very puzzled expression on her face.

"Sorry, Michael. I didn't realise you were in a trance ... I gave this book to Ernest and asked him to tell me what it was. He looked at it, then he seemed very surprised. He wouldn't tell me about it. He told me to ask you. Don't you think that is odd?"

Michael stood up and automatically pushed *A Short History of the World* in his pocket.

He took the book that Emily held out and shone his torch on the title page.

Hesitantly but accurately, he read: *"Wuthering Heights by Emily Brontë."*

SIXTEEN

Michael gazed at the book in his hand as if it might explode. Emily Brontë! It had never occurred to him—so many things had never occurred to him—that there could be more than one Emily Brontë. And that this other Emily could be sufficiently clever to create a book consisting of thousands and thousands of words—the knowledge confounded him.

He opened the book and shone his torch on a page headed Chapter One. Then, with some difficulty, and making a mess of words such as neighbour and situation, he read the first few sentences aloud:

"I have just returned from a visit to my landlord—the solitary neighbour that I shall be troubled with. This is certainly a beautiful country. In all England, I do not believe that I could have fixed on a situation so completely removed from the stir of society."

He closed the book and looked wonderingly at the Emily Brontë who now stood by his side.

"What does it mean?" she asked.

"I don't know. I would have to read more words and get familiar with the way they are being used."

"I don't mean the book. How does someone else come to have my name? I thought names were special."

Michael sighed. "I don't know that, either ... Sorry, Emily. I'm the expert on not knowing ... I don't know why but I never imagined that more than one person would have the same name." He laughed bitterly. "For all I know, there could be a large number of Emily Brontës somewhere. I only specialise in ignorance."

"Perhaps she is dead," suggested Ernest.

"Who?"

"The Emily Brontë who made the book. It looks a very old book. She could have died a long time ago."

"I suppose so."

"Perhaps," said Emily, "perhaps there is some reason— some link between my name and her name."

"I wonder if she was a fragile," said Horatio. "Probably not. Not if she could read and write and put a lot of big words together to make a book ... I bet she—it—was one hell of a drybone."

Michael had a sudden, intuitive conviction. "She was not a drybone. None of the people who wrote these books were drybones. The drybones don't care about reading and writing. They don't *need* books. Only fragiles need books or care about them." He was suddenly inspired. "We have company, here. Company of our own kind. A company of minds. Now that we have found books, we will all learn to read properly. Then we shall be able to understand what these other fragiles thought and hoped and did ... Emily is right, though. There may be some link."

"Let's look for names," said Ernest. "We had better

look together. It is too dark now to see clearly without the torch."

Horatio was beginning to be bored. "While you people look for names, I'll nose around and see if there is anything else of interest ... I don't think you are going to get much out of these books."

Although Emily and Jane were not sufficiently skilled even at recognising instantly all the different letter shapes, they stayed close to Michael and Ernest, scanning the piles of books in the hope that, somehow, something would be revealed to them.

It was quite a time before the next discovery was made. The darkness in the sky, seen through the library's grimy windows, was no longer the darkness of storm clouds but of approaching evening.

Appropriately, it was Ernest who saw the book first and instantly recognised a word that seemed to leap out at him. The word was Rutherford, and it was the title of the book.

"*Rutherford!*" Ernest spoke the word as if he were using it for the first time. He opened the book and looked at the first printed page. Under the title he read: *"Being an account of the life and work of Ernest Rutherford, Baron Rutherford of Nelson, O.M., scientist and genius."*

"Rutherford," echoed Michael. "Scientist and genius ... First Emily Brontë, now Ernest Rutherford ... Do all our names also belong to other fragiles?" He sighed. "There are so many books to look at. We shall have to come back here again and again. I was so eager to get hold of some books, but now that we have found them I'm almost terrified."

Jane had a curious thought. "I wonder if these other fragiles could be related to Ernest and Emily?" She hesitated. "The drybones are supposed to be our parents, but they are not at all like us ... It is a silly thought, but could these other fragiles belong in some way to Emily and Ernest?"

There was a silence. Eventually, Michael spoke. "I'll tell you what I think. I think the people who made these books—all of them—are our true parents. I think the dry-bones want to keep us from learning the truth about ourselves because the truth is to their disadvantage."

Everyone had forgotten about Horatio. They heard his voice. It sounded far away.

"Bring the torch," he called. "I have lost my sense of direction in the darkness."

"Where are you?"

"There is a door at the far end of the library, with steps leading down. I went down them. Now I can't see which way to get back up."

Michael led the way. The torch battery was losing power. The light given out was now a pale orange instead of bright yellow. Besides the entrance, there were three other doors in the library. Only one of them was open, and it was obviously the door Horatio had used.

The flight of steps was steep and long. Michael was surprised that Horatio had not fallen down in the darkness and hurt himself. Even with the light, he and the others had to move carefully. They found Horatio in one of the two passageways leading from the foot of the steps. The walls of each were bare, and no provision had been made for electric lighting. But the really surprising thing was that these subterranean corridors seemed to reach far beyond the confines of the library, perhaps even beyond Apollo Twelve Square.

Michael and the others tried to explore the corridor in which Horatio was and find out where it ended. They walked along it for some time; and Ernest estimated that, in terms of distance, they must be half-way back to Picca-dilly Circus. But by then the torch was getting very low indeed, and Michael would not risk stranding the Family in darkness.

Without discovering any end to the passages or any evidence of the purpose or purposes for which they had been built, the Family made its way back to the library. It was almost as dark in the large room as in the underground passages.

Emily slipped her hand into Michael's. "I don't think I ought to stay any longer. I promised Mother I would be home early. We are supposed to be going to the pictures."

"There isn't much point in any of us staying without light," said Michael. "We shall have to come again, properly equipped."

Horatio was excited. "The passages have to go some-where. I think it might be somewhere important. They can't just go round in circles."

"They could," said Ernest. "But I have a feeling they don't. We may have found something besides the books that the drybones don't want us to find yet."

Michael regarded the pale glow of his torch sadly. "It will keep. Let us get one or two books while we can still see something. Then we'll all go together."

They had to shine the torch very close to the spines of the books to read the titles.

Michael already had *A Short History of the World.* He was lucky enough to find another relevant book *A History of England* in the same pile. Ernest took *Rutherford, The Concise Oxford Dictionary of English Literature*, which he had literally tumbled over, and *Utopia.* Emily kept *Wuthering Heights.* Jane found *The Jungle Book.* Horatio took nothing. He could not read. He did not want to learn to read. If there was anything important in books, Michael or Ernest would be sure to tell him.

The light from the torch was now so weak that they had to hold hands and feel their way out of the library. The rain had stopped. The wind had died down. The night air was cool and clean.

Michael and Ernest were filled with great excitement. At last they had found something to read.

SEVENTEEN

Michael hid his books in the bathroom. It seemed the best and safest place. The bath had panelled sides, and the small end panel was only held in position by two recessed screws. They were very loose and could be unscrewed by a nail file.

Of course, it would have been possible to keep the books openly in his room. He tried to analyse why he didn't. It was more than the fear of losing them. It was fear of having the drybones discover that he now had a source of information other than radio, television or Father's evasive explanations.

A Short History of the World was a formidable book. It contained a large number of words he could not pronounce or knew he was pronouncing wrongly and a large number of words whose meaning he could only guess. The Contents list gave him an idea of the chapters that would be of most interest. Indeed, the Contents list itself was a kind of distilled history, ranging from fascinating headings such

as "The Beginnings of Life" and "The First True Men"
to "The Industrial Revolution" and "The Second World
War".

Each session that Michael spent with his books was an
exhausting session of revelation. He would lock himself in
the bathroom, run the bath water and, while it was running
noisily, unscrew the panel with his nail file. As the room
filled with steam, he would make shattering discoveries,
which sometimes brought such mental confusion that his
head ached and he longed desperately to ask questions of
someone who *knew*.

But there was no one to answer the questions. He must
answer his own or seek answers in the daunting pages of
the book. Michael had no doubt that the truth—or as much
of it as could be ascertained—was contained in the pages
of his two books. Sometimes he was able to check information contained in one against information contained in the
other. He was not surprised when the books agreed. He
was only surprised when they appeared to disagree.

In neither of the books did he find any reference to drybones and fragiles as two distinct races. He found only
references to people—people who lived and died in
strange and sometimes appalling circumstances. But he
made discoveries that exploded like bombs in his mind.

He discovered that Queen Victoria was already dead,
that Sir Winston Churchill had never been her prime
minister, that the Second World War had already ended,
that London should be a vast, thriving city containing
millions of people. There was no mention of the exploration of the moon, or the American expedition to Mars, or
force fields to protect capital cities, or even the Overman
legend.

What to believe? The apparent reality of the world in
which he lived or the world described in two astounding

books? At times, torn by uncertainty, he began to think that Mother and Father might be right. The truth—the truth about anything—might be too terrible, too dangerous for fragiles to face. Perhaps the drybones really were protecting all fragiles—protecting them from realities too horrible to contemplate.

But then he would turn to *A Short History of the World* or *A History of England*; and the direct statements, the matching of information, would convince him that truth lay more in those printed words than in the apparent realities that surrounded him.

Michael had not had nightmares for some time; but now they came back. One night he woke up screaming, and Mother tried to comfort him as she had done when he was a small child. But there was no comfort in her arms, only an intensified horror of contact with a drybone.

Father said he looked ill and asked what was worrying him. For a dreadful moment, Michael had an impulse to confess all. Even the act of confession might ease the pressure, reduce the tension, no matter what Father said or did. But Michael squashed the impulse, squashed it for ever.

Somehow he knew that the authors of the books he had been reading were his own kind, fragiles. Somehow, he knew that their world was real and his was not. Somehow, he knew that Mother and Father and all the other drybones were jailers—jailers for a small group of fragiles whose only hope of survival lay in finding reality and accepting it.

So he said nothing. He locked himself in with his books, struggling to separate fantasy from fact in a tiny steam-filled room. He forced himself to believe that he was sane and that truth should be pursued for its own sake. He tried to act normally and to do the things that were expected of him. Above all, he was determined to conceal his new-found knowledge from everyone but the Family. His reading revealed that books had once been considered dangerous weapons, that they had been burnt or destroyed, and that their writers and readers had been persecuted. Perhaps he was living now in a world where books were still dangerous weapons. If so, he would arm himself. He would arm himself with ideas.

One evening, Michael went to the bathroom and locked himself in as usual. He turned the bath taps on and unscrewed the panel.

The books had gone.

For a moment or two he was stunned. Then he carefully replaced the panel and sat on the side of the bath to think.

So they had known. They had known all the time. He felt stupid and childish, and his cheeks burned with humiliation. They had demonstrated that he was still a child and they were still the masters. Briefly, he wanted to die.

But then ... But then he found some bitter consolation. They could not know how much he already knew or suspected. Even if they contrived to remove all the books from London Library, they still could not remove the knowledge already stored in his head. That was something.

Michael did not mention the books to Mother and Father. They did not mention the books to him. He determined to visit the library again as soon as possible.

EIGHTEEN

On Saturday evening, Ernest and Michael stole two bicycles from a number that were racked in the bicycle stands outside the Odeon cinema in Leicester Square. They took the bicycles to the stands outside Westminster Abbey and left them there. Early on Sunday morning they met at the Abbey, each with enough food for the day. It was to be a day of mechanised exploration.

They had taught themselves to ride secretly. For some time Father had promised that it would not be long before Michael would be allowed to use a bicycle. But, as usual, there were always good reasons why it could not be now; and Michael soon realised that he would have to do something about it himself. Ernest had also suffered the delay treatment. Bicycles were precious because there was a war on, and they should only be used by responsible adults.

So Ernest and Michael had taught themselves to ride

on the few occasions when a bicycle was available and no drybone owner was in sight.

Sunday morning was cold but fine. The rendezvous at Westminster Abbey took place before the first service. Michael realised that he and Ernest would be very conspicuous; but he thought they had a good chance of getting out of central London without being recognised by anyone who knew them.

They were both excited. Ernest was still convinced that, like the Thames, all the roads apparently leading out of London would bend back upon themselves. Michael was not so sure. He thought there must be some way of getting completely out of London.

They cycled over Westminster Bridge, meeting no one. In fact they met no one all day—which was, as Ernest put it, statistically absurd.

The first spell of riding, which gave them an appetite for breakfast, took them well away from the parts of London they knew. The road was lined with houses, shops, cafés, gardens. It crossed other, similar roads. But nowhere were there any signs of drybones or fragiles. Michael was reminded of the ghost-towns he had seen in Westerns. There was only a great sense of emptiness.

They stopped for breakfast at a coffee house. The door was open but the coffee house was empty. There was dust everywhere. It looked as if it had not been used for years.

"We are still in the country of the mad," observed Ernest grimly. "And I feel crazy enough to be sane. Let us go through the whole place and see if we can find anything."

They found two empty rooms upstairs—empty even of furniture—and a high-walled overgrown garden at the back. They sat in the garden, eating bread and cheese and talking. They talked about what they had learned from the books they had found.

"That other Ernest Rutherford was a very brilliant man," said Ernest. "Without his work in atomic physics, nuclear energy could never have been achieved."

Michael looked at him blankly. "Atomic physics? Nuclear energy? What is it all about?"

Ernest sighed. "I hardly know myself. Except that they are real. They can't be anything else but real. The experiments he carried out, the results he achieved are too—too elegant for invention."

"Elegance!" Michael laughed harshly. "I have some elegant notions for you. This vast, empty London that we live in contains millions of people. The books say so. Queen Victoria died long before the war we are now having—which also ended some time ago—began. The books say so. London was bombed frequently. Lots of people were killed and many buildings were destroyed. The books say so."

Ernest was silent for a time. Then he said: "We are real, the facts in the books are real. The London we live in is real. But ..."

"But this London is not *the* London," said Michael. "This Queen Victoria—a drybone, no doubt—is not *the* Queen Victoria ... It is all—all a bad model."

"Or," added Ernest, "a model with the inaccuracies carefully designed ... Sometimes, Michael, I think we are not on Earth at all. I am reduced to seeking the truth in fantasy. Sometimes, I think that space raiders came and captured us as babies. They took us back to their home planet and tried to create a natural environment for us. But they made some things wrong—by accident or by design."

Michael did not laugh or even smile. He considered the

notion seriously. At last he said: "I doubt if space travel exists. The books did not mention it."

"It may not have existed for Earth people," Ernest pointed out. "But there is no reason why it should not exist for other creatures elsewhere."

"Drybones?"

"Possibly."

"Come on," said Michael, standing up. "There is a lot to do. We can play with our theories tomorrow. Before we set off again, let's take a look at some of the houses along the road. I imagine they will be just as derelict as this place."

None of the doors were locked, and the houses were as Michael anticipated—empty, dusty, unlived in. Shells. Ghost-town houses. Presently, Ernest and Michael took their bicycles and rode on. Before lunch, they could already see the recognisable skyline of central London in the distance. They found they were heading for Black-friars Bridge.

After lunch, they took a different road. It looked much the same as the first one—in fact, at one point Ernest thought he recognised a particular sequence of houses— but this time they were returned to Chelsea Bridge. By then it was late afternoon, and they were both fairly tired. They rested a little and ate the last of their food.

"One more try," said Michael. "I think I know what the result will be. But we shall have the advantage of getting the bicycles back in darkness."

It was quite dark before they discovered where the road they chose had finally taken them. Ernest, though more tired than Michael and very saddle-sore, seemed to be vastly amused when he recognised the approach to Westminster Bridge.

"In our beginning is our end," he said, almost happily.

"In our end is our beginning."

"Did you invent that?"

"No. I borrowed it from a book."

Michael was suddenly struck by a thought. "We can't keep the bicycles. Why don't we put them back where we found them, at the Odeon?"

"We may be seen."

"A risk worth taking. After seeing no one all day I'll be almost glad to meet a drybone."

But, curiously, they managed to get the bicycles back to the Odeon, Leicester Square, without encountering either fragiles or drybones.

It had been an unnerving kind of day—a day in which, at times, they had felt like the only people left alive.

Before they parted, to return to their own homes, Ernest brought up once more the question of Michael's disappearing books. He had not shown a great deal of surprise when Michael had first told him what had happened. So far he had been lucky. His books, wrapped in plastic sheet, were hidden in the shrubbery in St. James's Park.

"I wonder how they knew where you kept them."

"What?"

"The books."

"I simply don't know. Maybe they are telepathic, these alien child stealers. Or maybe there is some way of seeing into the bathroom. Or maybe one of the screws in the wretched panel fell out. Does it matter?"

Ernest put a reassuring arm on his shoulder. "I don't think so. If they were going to do anything about it, they would have done it by now."

"I'm going back to the library tomorrow night. Then we will know."

"Would you like me to come?"

Michael shook his head. "It is better alone. They may not know if anyone else has taken books."

Ernest said tangentially: "We are not on Earth, you know. Suddenly, I am sure of it."

"What makes you so sure?"

"Mad logic. Quite mad logic. All those rows of deserted houses, this whole situation."

It was a cold clear night. The wind had begun to blow. Michael looked up at the unchanging pattern of the stars and shivered. They, at least, were constants. He wondered if, really, the Earth were somewhere out there. He wondered if in some far reach of space, there was another London—a real London, unimaginably crowded with people, where a river ran to the sea and where roads led to other towns and cities.

"Mad logic indeed," he said, "but either not mad enough or else too mad to justify that extravagance."

Ernest also was shivering—with fatigue, with coldness, with excitement. "I've saved the maddest bit to the last," he said, his teeth chattering a little. "One of my books— *The Concise Oxford Dictionary of English Literature*. It has in it the names of more than half the fragiles we know ... Michael, I'm cold. I'm cold so that I'll never be warm again. You know the coldness I mean?"

"I know it," said Michael softly. "I know it."

NINETEEN

Oddly, the library was less dark than when Michael and the Family had last been there. Outside, the sky had only a few thin skeins of cloud, and most of the stars were brilliant, sharp, untwinkling. The full moon was bright with cold fire; its light strong enough to penetrate the dusty library windows, supplying a ghostly illumination to the piles of books.

Michael found the scene disturbing and enchanting. Beautiful. Like the set for a romantic film. Like a symbol of life in the midst of death. For here were the strange, world-shattering thoughts of hundreds of fragiles committed to countless bound sheets of paper.

There was something wonderful about books. Something elegant. They could preserve thoughts and ideas for ever—or as long as paper would last. They were devices for allowing the human spirit to leap across time and space. They were the most marvellous, the most fascinating things in the world.

He was amused at his own mute eloquence. He had not come here to rhapsodise about books, but to find one or two that might provide more information. He looked around carefully. Nothing seemed to have been disturbed since the last time.

He took the torch out of his pocket—he had got a new battery for it from Father's store cupboard—pressed the switch, and allowed the beam of artificial light to reinforce the moonlight. He became more confident that nothing had been disturbed since last time. Except that the door at the far end of the library, the one that led down to the passages, was open. Michael could not remember whether anyone had shut it when they left the library before.

He switched off the torch, reluctant to challenge the moonlight, reluctant even to disturb the stillness by moving. He wished Emily was with him. He wanted her to be with him very much. Apart from brief periods at high school and the reading lessons he gave her, usually with Jane Austen, he had not had any time alone with her for several days.

He and Emily had become very dependent upon each other. They kissed and caressed. They said foolish things that did not seem foolish at all at the time. They explored each other's bodies and found them exciting. They discovered how each other's secret parts could be aroused to intense feeling. Michael had found that, in the end, it was only reasonable that such secret parts should be brought together, and the intensity doubled, tripled, quadrupled until there was nothing but unthinking ecstasy.

The first time he had thus held and loved Emily was by moonlight, by summer moonlight among tall, feathery grasses. He wished that she was here now. He badly wanted to hold her and love her, here among the books

100

with moonlight on her face, among the silent thoughts and words of all those other fragiles.

Away with thoughts of Emily. He had come for books. He switched on the torch once more and began to inspect his treasure.

The first pile he explored seemed to consist entirely of long stories: *Sons and Lovers* by D. H. Lawrence; *For Whom The Bell Tolls* by Ernest Hemingway; *The Green Child* by Herbert Read; *The Lost Horizon* by James Hilton; and *The Grapes of Wrath* by John Steinbeck.

Michael flipped the pages of some of them, reading a paragraph here and there. His reading was good now. He could read quickly without stumbling much over the big words. There were still many words and expressions that he did not understand; but not enough to severely distort the meaning of what he read.

He found some of the fragments that he read fascinating; but at the moment he wanted something more useful than stories. One day, perhaps, there would be time for stories. But now the need was for information. Regretfully, he put the books down and turned to another pile. That, too, proved to be stories.

He wandered about, glancing at several such piles, until the torch beam shone on four books, similarly bound. The titles and the name of the author seemed to have a physical impact upon him. The books were four volumes of a history of the Second World War, and the author was Winston Churchill. The titles of the volumes were: *The Gathering Storm, Their Finest Hour, The Grand Alliance* and *The Hinge of Fate*.

Michael picked up *The Gathering Storm* and began to flip through the pages, snatching a subtitle and a sentence or two here and there. His excitement increased. These were the kind of books he needed—books that gave a real account of what had happened in a real world. But where could he possibly hide four such substantial books? Certainly not at home. It looked as if he would be reduced to using some hiding place similar to Ernest's; but then he would not be able to read as frequently as he wished.

However, the thing to do was to take the books and try to work out where to hide them on the way back home. Michael switched off the torch and put it in his pocket. Then he picked up the books and, after a few moments of savouring once more the combination of moonlight and books, he turned to go.

Suddenly he froze. He could hear a noise—the sound of running feet. It seemed to be coming from the open doorway at the far end of the library. The doorway that led down to those enigmatic underground passages.

Michael could have hidden, he could have gone quickly out of the library. But he just stood there, waiting, wondering if the drybones were now springing a carefully laid trap.

It was indeed a drybone who ran up the steps, through the doorway and into the library. But there was the sound of more running feet, hard behind.

Michael recognised the drybone instantly. It was Aldous Huxley, who had tried to make friends with the Family in the Strand Coffee House, one Saturday morning.

The recognition was mutual. Aldous Huxley stopped running just as his pursuer emerged from the doorway. It was Horatio.

"So you have both discovered—" began Aldous Huxley. But the sentence was never finished.

Horatio had his iron bar. With a great cry of rage or anguish, he rushed at the drybone and savagely brought the iron bar down on his head. There was a curious, breaking noise.

Aldous Huxley did not immediately fall, as any fragile would have done on receiving such a vicious blow. He jerked, spasmodically, uttered a high, piercing whine, then with curious, jerky movements apparently tried to walk through the library wall.

Michael watched, paralysed with shock.

Horatio was beside himself. He hit Aldous Huxley again and again with the iron bar. The drybone made no effort to defend himself. He just tried to claw and scrabble his way through the library wall.

But the rain of heavy blows was too much even for a drybone. Suddenly he fell down, and lay on the floor, jerking and twisting.

Michael was still paralysed. Horatio paid no attention to him. He was berserk.

The thing on the floor was still whining. Horatio, sobbing and screaming, lifted his iron bar with both hands and put all his weight and strength into a last, terrible blow.

There was a sickening crunch. Then Aldous Huxley's head, or what was left of it, went spinning across the library floor. The body stopped jerking. Horatio dropped the iron bar and crumpled up, moaning and crying, hiding his face in his hands.

Though he felt numb with shock, movement was restored to Michael's body. Without thinking, he went across to where Aldous Huxley's head lay, by a pile of books.

The skull, face and neck were smashed, grotesquely distorted. But there was no blood. The neck, abnormally long, had ragged edges where the skin had been torn. But there was no blood.

Michael wanted to be sick. But Horatio was hysterical, and something would have to be done about the body, and there was no time to be sick. Perhaps he could allow himself the luxury of being sick later. Michael fought the nausea back, pulled the torch out of his pocket and willed himself to bend down and inspect the head.

There was no blood, none at all. But inside the base of the neck, where the skin was torn in a ragged circle, there seemed to be a kind of black plate. Protruding from the plate was a number of sturdy metal pins, some bent, perhaps by Horatio's furious onslaught.

There was nothing to be done for Aldous Huxley.

Horatio still lay curled up with his hands over his eyes, still moaning and keening like a terrified child.

Michael went and knelt by him, putting an arm round his shoulder, holding him and trying to calm him down.

"What happened, Horatio?" he asked gently. "Try to tell me what happened."

Horatio didn't answer. He just continued to shake and cry. Michael's arm tightened round his shoulders, trying to steady him.

Presently Michael tried again. "You must tell me what happened, Horatio. I have to think what to do."

"It was the lizards, the great lizards!" sobbed Horatio. "They scared me out of my mind, and I started to run back, and I bumped into ... into ... and I thought ... I thought he would ..." The effort to be rational was too much, and Horatio's body shook convulsively.

Michael continued to hold him, trying to be patient, trying to think, while the cold fire of moonlight bathed the untidy piles of books and the sightless head of the drybone.

TWENTY

It took a long time to get Horatio sensible once more. Too long. Michael would have to think of some convincing fabrications before he returned home. So, he realised, would Horatio. Michael wondered how he would stand up to the inevitable questioning of his parents.

But that was not an immediate problem. The immediate problems were to restore Horatio's spirit, to find out exactly what had happened, and to do something about what was left of Aldous Huxley. One thing was certain: his remains could not be allowed to stay in the library. Their discovery would be a threat to the entire Family.

With patience and gentleness and an air of confidence he did not really feel, Michael tried to reassure Horatio and to convince him that, if they both kept their heads, everything would turn out all right.

Presently, Horatio recovered sufficiently to be able to uncover his face and look at what he had done. His face was still wet; but the tears and the moaning had stopped, and all that remained of his recent hysteria was a rhythmic and convulsive sighing—like the laboured breathing of someone who had made great exertions.

Horatio surveyed the body almost calmly. He looked at the black, perforated plate set deep between the shoulders, its holes corresponding to the pattern of pins in the plate at the base of the neck.

"So that is how they are joined together," said Horatio. "What do you think we would find if we opened up the body—lots of little motors and wires and valves, like in an old radio?"

"I don't know," said Michael. "But we are not going to find out. You had better tell me what happened, and then we will have to decide what to do about—about the pieces."

Horatio did not seem to hear him. He was studying Aldous Huxley's head and the bent pins in the black plate. "Michael, look at this. I have just had an idea. Wouldn't it be possible for one drybone to have several different heads—or for one drybone head to have several different bodies? The skin is torn because—because of what I did. But there must be a way of sealing and un-sealing it."

"Horatio, we can't consider all the implications now. There will be plenty of time to think about them later—if we can successfully get ourselves out of this mess."

Again Horatio appeared not to have heard him. "That would explain how the drybones at school tried to keep pace with our growing," he said excitedly. "I've noticed them very carefully. They don't grow evenly as we do. They seem to stay the same size for a long time, then suddenly shoot up an inch or so overnight." He laughed, and the edge of hysteria was still evident in his voice. "Of course. They do it by changing their bodies. I must explore Ellen Terry's body very thoroughly next time I see her, to make sure she isn't wearing a boy's body by mistake."

The laughter became higher in pitch. Michael took hold of Horatio and shook him hard. But that didn't stop it. So Michael slapped him hard, very hard. And the pain brought him back to his senses.

"I'm sorry, Michael ... I've made a hell of a mess of it, haven't I? Now there is going to be real trouble."

"Listen," said Michael fiercely. "There isn't time to be sorry. There isn't time to speculate on the nature of drybones. You must tell me as quickly as possible what has happened."

Horatio pulled himself together and gave his account. After he had first discovered the underground passage, he had become convinced that it would lead out of London; and he determined to explore it as soon as he had an opportunity. He said nothing to Michael and Ernest because they had seemed engrossed in their wretched books, and he had sensed that they would probably want to delay exploration for a while until they found out what, if anything, the books revealed.

"Also," confessed Horatio disarmingly, "I wanted to do something on my own ... I'm not very good at being told what to do, Michael. You must have realised that. Besides, I wanted to be able to find out something useful and then come to you and say: Look! Surprise, surprise!"

"Well, you did that." Michael's voice was grim. "You did exactly that."

Horatio had risked coming to the library in mid-afternoon. He had with him his iron bar and an electric torch with new batteries. He walked round Apollo Twelve Square twice before he entered the library, trying to make sure that he was not followed. Horatio was certain, in fact, that he had not been followed and that Aldous Huxley must have already been in the library when he arrived.

"If there had been any sign of a drybone anywhere, I would have abandoned the stunt. But the situation seemed absolutely perfect."

"Too perfect," observed Michael. He glanced at what was left of Aldous Huxley. "We can only hope that this one was here casually ... Which of the passageways did you take—the one we found you in last time?"

"Yes. I knew it was going to be a long job because of last time. I thought I'd save the other one until you and Ernest were present ... I waited in the library for a while before I went down the stairs, just listening to make sure I was alone. But there wasn't the slightest sound. The whole place was dead."

Michael sighed. "Which leads to the nasty thought that if Aldous Huxley was already present, he was hiding. And if he was hiding, he was doing it for a purpose."

"But he couldn't have known that we had found the library."

"Possibly. But he could have known that *some* fragiles had found the library."

Horatio had gone down the stairs, switched his torch on and had begun to walk along his chosen passage as fast as possible. He wanted to get to the end of it quickly not just because he was impatient to discover where it led but also because he wanted to return home before his absence excited too much interest.

The corridor was long and slightly curved. It also seemed to be sloping downwards. The walls, roof and floor were monotonously smooth and were rather damp in places. Horatio noticed that his footsteps echoed. After a time he alternated periods of walking with periods of running. He had just finished one period of sustained running and was taking a short rest when he became aware that the echoes of his footsteps were apparently continuing. Oddly, it did not occur to him at that point that anyone else could be in the corridor. He simply concluded that it must be so long that the sound of his footsteps was reverberating along it.

However, some time later he took another rest and listened once more to the apparent echoes. That was when he noticed that the rhythm was different from the rhythm of his own footsteps.

"I didn't panic, Michael. At first I thought it might be you or Ernest, having had the same idea that I had. But I thought the best thing to do would be to press on and reach the end of the passage. I imagined it might be possible to conceal myself somewhere; and if whoever was behind me turned out to be you, we could have a laugh about frightening each other because you—or he—must have been hearing my footsteps, too ... If it was a drybone, then I'd just keep out of the way and try to see who it was. That was the theory."

"The practice?"

Horatio shuddered. "The practice was different ... I don't know what I thought would be at the end of the passage. I don't know what I thought it would be like outside London. I suppose I imagined fields and villages and hills and woods—that kind of thing ... It had been a long journey. I—I came to the door and ..." Horatio stopped, obviously agitated by the memory and obviously trying to control himself. "And—and I just wasn't prepared for it ... I'm sorry, Michael."

Michael put a hand on his shoulder. "Take it easy, Horatio. Nobody doubts your courage."

"It was just an ordinary door ... Just an ordinary door. Unlocked. I—I turned the handle and opened it ..."

Horatio put his hand to his forehead and pressed hard, as if he were trying to press back nightmares, phantoms. "There were rocks, great rocks and a roaring of water. And there were these things—I was too shaken to see what they were at first—these huge lizards ... And there was one very near. It turned its head and looked at me ... I think I must have screamed, because they all looked. Then I slammed the door and I ran. God, how I ran! I think I was still screaming. Then I heard the footsteps coming towards me. And somebody was calling. And then I ran into the drybone ... I—I went to pieces. I thought he was going to kill me or drive me back to the lizards. So I knocked him down and hit him as hard as I could. But he managed to get up somehow, and I chased him all the way back. I had to smash him then—for a different reason. He would tell the others, and then you and Ernest might be drawn in ... and ... and ... *Michael, I had to smash something!*"

Horatio was shouting and sobbing once more.

"Yes, you had to smash something," said Michael sadly, again holding Horatio and soothing him like a child.

This time the hysteria wore off quite quickly, and then Horatio became abnormally calm. "What a jaunt," he said. "This will shake the Family, won't it, Michael?"

Michael felt depressed and afraid. "Yes, this will shake the Family."

"Did I do wrong to smash the drybone? He could have been very dangerous."

"I don't know. I just don't know ... Listen, Horatio, this is what we are going to do now. We are going to pick up the—the pieces and take them down into the passage. We'll take them along it as far as we can without using up too much time. Then tomorrow night Ernest and I will dispose of them."

The body was no heavier than the body of a fragile. Michael and Horatio manhandled it down the steps and dragged it about a hundred paces along the corridor. Then they went back up into the library.

"Stay here," said Michael, "and don't do a thing." He went to pick up the battered head. It was heavier than he thought. Heavier than the head of a fragile, probably.

But it wasn't the head of a fragile. It was the head of a —a machine. Michael felt sick and numb. Because the machine had been demonstrably a person, and the person was now no more. He avoided looking at the head as much as possible. But the hair felt absurdly soft in his hands, and the skin felt like ordinary skin, but hard and cool. With an immense effort of will, he managed to carry it down the steps and along the corridor. For reasons that he could not understand, he tried gently to fix it on to the body. But the pins were all bent and it wouldn't fit.

By the time he got back into the library, Horatio seemed in remarkably good spirits. "At least, that's one less we have to worry about. What is the programme now, Michael? I suppose we ought to go home."

"Yes, we must go home as fast as we can. You'd better invent a good story, Horatio."

"Don't worry. Don't worry. They are used to me being unpredictable. I often tell them to go to hell anyway ... Tomorrow night, Michael, you and Ernest will need help to get rid of the bits. I can—"

"You have done enough already," cut in Michael. "You had better keep out of mischief for a day or two."

"How are you going to dispose of the remains, then?"

Michael thought for a moment or two. "I don't like it a bit," he said grimly. "But about the safest thing I can think of is to make a free gift to those lizards."

TWENTY-ONE

Michael and Ernest were not able to go to the library on the following night. They were not able to go until three nights later. The first evening was taken up by an invitation—which Michael had forgotten—from Mr. and Mrs. Brontë to Mr. and Mrs. Faraday and Michael to play Monopoly. Since everyone was well aware of the situation between Emily and Michael, it would have looked exceedingly odd if he had evaded this opportunity of seeing her.

The second evening was taken up by an exhibition of students' work at high school. All students were expected to attend, along with their parents, if possible. And it was a foregone conclusion that all the drybone parents would want to see what their children had been doing. Michael had an intricate model of Westminster Abbey on show. Ernest had done a series of paintings of British military aircraft.

The third evening, however, was free. Michael, Ernest

and Horatio waited for it with impatience and dread. Horatio seemed to have recovered from his horrifying experience and pleaded to be allowed to help dispose of the wreckage of Aldous Huxley. He promised never again to undertake any private exploration without Michael's consent. In the end, Michael decided that it was probably safer and wiser to have Horatio present than to leave him out of the disposal operation. It was going to be a hard task hauling Aldous Huxley along the passage to that tantalising door to the outside world. Three people would obviously do the job a great deal faster than two.

Michael had told Ernest all that had happened, but he had told no one else—not even Emily. The fewer the people who knew about the bizarre situation the better. Nevertheless, Michael had a depressing conviction that it was not going to be possible to restrict the knowledge of the destruction of Aldous Huxley to three fragiles.

He was right.

They arrived at the library when dusk was beginning to blend into darkness. Apollo Twelve Square, as on previous occasions, was deserted. All seemed entirely normal, but Michael sensed that something was wrong.

Inside the library, they discreetly used one of the torches they had brought. Nothing seemed to have been disturbed. The Winston Churchill books lay where Michael had put them down—the shock of Aldous Huxley's destruction had driven them completely from his mind, and he was only now reminded of their existence. He determined not to forget them this time when he left. A history of the Second World War—the one that was still supposed to be going on—was something he greatly looked forward to reading.

"We are in luck," said Horatio, relief in his voice. "No one seems to have been here."

"I hope we are in luck," said Michael grimly. He didn't believe it.

After a cursory inspection, they went down the steps and along the passage to where Aldous Huxley's head and body had been laid. They weren't there. Michael was surprised that he felt no surprise; and then he realised that this was exactly what he had expected. He wondered why.

Horatio, the tough one, began to panic again. "We have got to get out," he insisted. "We have got to get out. They have turned it into a trap!" He shone his torch in agitation up and down the passage as if he expected to be rushed by drybones at any minute.

"If it is a trap," said Ernest quietly, "we are already inside it. Calm yourself, Horatio. Rushing about and flashing lights all over the place is not going to do any good ... Well, Michael, you are the general. What do we do?"

"It is not a trap," said Michael. "At least, it is not a trap in the sense of being designed to catch us."

"How do you know?"

"I can't explain. But in some way, I am beginning to discern a pattern ... It is as if we are in some kind of war or elaborate game. Our opponents—the drybones—try to defeat us or divert us by a constant application of the unexpected. A trap is therefore now expected. You see what I mean?"

"I think so. But what do we do?"

Horatio groaned. "While you two blather, the library is probably being surrounded by drybones. Let us try to get out before it is too late."

"If your theory were correct, Horatio, it would already be too late ... We were going to dump Aldous Huxley in this terrifying outside world that Horatio glimpsed. No drybone. But let us not waste our opportunity. I want to see what is on the other side of that door. Can you face it again, Horatio?"

"Yes, but—"

"Then let us not waste any time. It is a long way there and back." Michael smiled. "One small consolation is that we are not now to be burdened by any heavy weight."

They followed Horatio's original method of travel— running for a spell, then walking until they had recovered their breath. Occasionally, they stood still in complete silence, listening for a time. But there were no sounds of pursuit.

Presently they came to the door. It did not look like a door leading into a nightmare world. It looked just like the kind of ordinary door that Horatio had described.

The journey along the passage had been even longer than Michael anticipated. All three of them were tired. He decided that they should take a little rest before look- ing outside. Wearily, all three of them sat down on the cold floor. Michael kept a torch switched on simply because the light provided an illusion of security.

"It will be dark out there," observed Ernest. "Probably we shall see nothing. Was it dark when you came, Horatio?"

"There was moonlight." Horatio shuddered. "I think the moonlight made it all look more terrible. Maybe it is not so bad in broad daylight."

"I took the trouble to check," said Michael. "It is full moon tonight ... You really are sure you can face it again, Horatio?"

"I managed it alone last time, didn't I?" snapped Horatio. "And I know what to expect now. Worry about yourself, Michael. Don't worry about me."

"Ssh!" said Ernest. "What is that noise?"

There was a muted, rhythmic roaring.

"Water," said Horatio. "Water against rocks."

Michael stood up. "Let's get it over. Whatever is out there, we can't stay long. We have to try to get back home at a reasonable hour."

He went to the door and turned the handle. As he opened the door, a great draught of cool, fresh air swept into the passageway. The roaring of the water became loud.

Michael opened the door wide.

Ernest and Horatio stood close by him. Michael suddenly felt as if he had received an electric shock. He heard Ernest draw in a great breath, noisily, unevenly. He heard Horatio utter a half-strangled cry.

There on the rocks lay Aldous Huxley.

TWENTY-TWO

Horatio had retreated into the passage. So had Ernest. Michael stood alone, surveying the world that was outside London.

"Come back," called Horatio. "Come back!"

"In a moment or two. If this is what the world is like, we have to know about it."

Michael looked around him.

The sky was clear, but the stars were pale against the brightness of a cold, yellow moon. Its light shed weird beauty on a landscape that seemed like a nightmare brought to the edge of reality.

The doorway was set in a sloping face of rock, sprinkled with huge boulders, and leading down to a thin strip of sand and pebbles and the breakers of a great sea. Further down among the rocks, far beyond the body of Aldous Huxley, there were shapes that were too smooth to be rocks. Some of them moved lazily. They were great moon-silvered lizards.

The hair rose on Michael's neck. His mouth became dry. His heart seemed to be trying to explode out of his chest.

He wanted to run back into the passage, slam the door and pretend that the fantastic world outside did not exist. But greater than the desire to retreat was the desire to stay, to learn about the nightmare that was real.

He stood there, waiting, watching, feeling the sea wind on his face, hearing the breakers on the rocks. Fear diminished a little. The lizards below, many of them nearly twice as long as Michael's own height, did not appear to be greatly interested in the vertical intruder. He waved his arms. The lizards noticed, and a few tails flicked indolently; but they took no further action. He shouted and clapped his hands. Silvery reptilian heads turned towards him. But when he stopped shouting and clapping, interest waned.

Fear diminished. Curiosity grew. Michael looked at the sea, the rocks, the lizards and the top of the ragged rock face, where grass and shrubs were growing. He wanted to explore further.

"Michael, come back!" Horatio spoke in a loud, hoarse, stage whisper, as if he was afraid of being overheard.

Michael went back into the passage and closed the door behind him. It was already hard to believe what lay on the other side of it.

"You have strong nerves," said Ernest. "I always knew you had. Shouldn't we be getting back?"

"We can spare a little more time," said Michael. "I want to go outside, really outside."

Horatio was appalled at the prospect. "They'll kill you —the lizards."

"I don't think so. They don't seem very interested."

"There is the matter of Aldous Huxley," began Ernest.

"I told you it was a trap," cut in Horatio. "By the time we get back, the place will be crawling with drybones."

Michael shook his head. "I think you are wrong. We are still caught up in the game of the unexpected. But even if there was a trap, that would strengthen the argument for exploring outside before we returned to walk into it."

"What do you want to do, Michael?" Ernest was trying to be calm, but could not keep a high note of anxiety out of his voice.

"Nothing spectacular, and it won't take long. I simply want to take a few steps outside. I'd like Horatio to stay here in the passage, holding the door open to prevent the wind slamming it and, perhaps, making it stick in some way. And I would like you, Ernest, to stand just outside the door with a couple of rocks ready to throw if the lizards become too inquisitive. I'll take a torch. It should dazzle any creature long enough to allow me to get back."

"I think you are crazy," said Horatio.

"I think you are intelligently crazy," amended Ernest. "Take my torch. It has the brightest beam."

The door was opened again. Horatio stood with his back pressed against it, peering apprehensively down the rock face. Ernest stepped out and found six or seven large fragments of rock. He built them into a neat little pile of ammunition at his feet.

Michael breathed the clean night wind and was exhilarated. He looked at the foaming edge of the sea, at the lizards, at the rocks, at the raw, raw world of reality. Absurdly, he wanted to sing. Out here it was strange and terrible. Out here was the danger of the unknown. But out here, also, he sensed freedom.

He smiled at Ernest, a pale, anxious ghost in moon-light.

"I won't be long."

"Be careful."

"Don't worry."

He put the torch in his pocket and began to climb up the rock face, away from the lizards, away from the sea. The going was hard. He had to use his hands. Pieces of rock were dislodged and rattled downwards. Something small scuttled between his legs. Wings flapped noisily on a ledge above, and there was the desolate cry of a bird.

Michael was shaking with excitement. Was this really the world of freedom? Or was all this still part of the kingdom of the drybones? Questions—always more questions. Enough to drive a man mad.

He had reached the top of the rock face now. There was grass beneath his feet; and here and there, silvery shrubs and bushes, small trees. The ground rose steeply to a hill, cutting off the view inland, stretching away left and right to where moonlight was defeated by misty darkness.

Michael was disappointed. He knew now what he had been hoping for. He had been hoping that he would be able to see London from the outside.

But the hill was high, and there was no time to climb it; and, anyway, he was too tired. He turned and looked down over the rocks towards the sea. Already, what at first had seemed terrible was now beautiful. Even the lizards, though still perhaps terrible, seemed beautiful.

Who could have imagined that an underground passage from a library in a city that was one colossal confidence trick could lead to this silver wilderness? London was not London. Perhaps Earth was not Earth. But the stars were real, and the lizards were real, and the ocean was a great water.

Michael was light-headed. He knew he should go back, but he was reluctant. He forced himself to scramble down the rocks to the door and the passage that led back to captivity.

Ernest and Horatio were visibly relieved at his return. There had been no trouble. The lizards had returned presumably to their slumbers.

"What did you see?"

"Just hills and coastline ... I have an idea this is wonderful country—here, outside ... Now, I suppose we must get back as quickly as possible."

"Into the trap," said Horatio gloomily. He closed the door carefully after they had all stepped back into the passage.

TWENTY-THREE

But, as Michael had predicted, there was no trap. The library was as they had left it. Michael remembered to pick up *The Second World War*. He still did not know where he was going to hide the heavy volumes; but he would think of that on the way home.

"It is terribly late," said Ernest. "Our drybone jailers are going to want explanations."

"We got lost," said Michael. "It is easy to get lost in London, isn't it? We were exploring together in North London and we got lost ... I'm beginning to think the drybones always know far more about our actions than we think they do. But let us stick to polite fictions—for the time being."

"Somebody knows about Aldous Huxley, at least," said Horatio gloomily.

Michael put a hand on his shoulder. "Try not to worry too much, Horatio. I'm sure they are playing with us; but there is one thing in our favour. I don't think they realise that we are turning into men and women."

"Let's go," said Ernest. "I could fall asleep on my feet."

Michael gave a last glance at the library. "There is just one other thing. For the next few days, we had better drop back into the role of retarded adolescents. This applies particularly to you, Horatio. O.K.?"

"Yes, master."

"Because," added Michael with unexpected intensity, "I will not have anyone stupidly endangering the Family or the rest of the fragiles. So, if you try any more free-lance operations, I might just kill you, Horatio. I mean it. Now don't say a damn thing."

Horatio was too surprised to offer comment.

For the next few days life went on normally. Or abnormally. Michael's parents had not required an explanation for his lateness in returning home. Indeed, when he got home, they were already in bed—an unusual occurrence. Father usually stayed up on such occasions to scold, make threats and demand an accounting. The following day, Michael learned that Horatio's parents and Ernest's parents had also been in bed when they returned. That, too, was curious. Part of the nightmare game, thought Michael. Part of the deadly game the drybones were playing in their disguise as teachers and parents.

He could not think of any safe place to hide the Winston Churchill books he had brought home; so in the end he hid them in the bathroom once more, behind the end panel of the bath. If his theory of the unexpected were true, the books would not be removed.

They were not removed. Indeed they were never re-moved until Michael himself took them back to the library. It confirmed his belief that he had learned something about drybone psychology.

Meanwhile, there was no hue and cry about Aldous

Huxley—which, also, was unexpected and now, therefore, to be expected. Whoever had taken his body and dumped it on the rocks by the sea seemed just as determined to conceal the operation as Michael was to conceal the fact of Aldous Huxley's destruction.

Sometimes, Michael felt that all the drybones in London must be quietly laughing at the ineptitude of the fragiles, at the childish attempts at exploration, at the furtive and futile concealments and plottings. Sometimes, in a fit of depression, he thought how much simpler it would be if only he could cauterise his curiosity, somehow close down the terrible need to understand. He had security, he lived in comfort, he could not be touched by the fake war the drybones had invented for reasons of their own.

Did it matter that London was a cardboard city? Did it matter that outside this enclosed world there was a greater world where lizards roamed and the sea battered endlessly against the rocks? Surely what mattered most was security. Even an animal in a zoo had security.

And that gave Michael his answer. He did not want the security of being an animal in a zoo. He wanted freedom in a real and natural world, however terrible or dangerous it might be. He knew then that he would risk anything to obtain that. Including his life.

TWENTY-FOUR

It was a warm, dark evening. Michael had obtained Mr. and Mrs. Brontë's permission to take Emily to an early showing of *The Man In The Iron Mask* at the Odeon, Leicester Square. And now, afterwards, they were walking hand in hand, deliciously alone in Green Park.

Emily had grown tall and beautiful. Her breasts were full and firm. She had more natural grace than any other fragile Michael knew. He was proud of her, he loved her, he desired her. Recently his need for her had become almost obsessional—perhaps because he was aware that the long years of innocence had gone; and that soon, people who had been conditioned to an endless childhood, would suddenly have to begin acting like and taking the decisions of men and women.

Michael had no secrets from Emily, partly because she was a member of the Family, but chiefly because he loved her. He never wanted to have thoughts in his head that he could not share with her. It would be a kind of cutting off.

"I want to kiss you," said Michael, loud enough to surprise himself.

"Then kiss me."

They held close together for a few moments, running their hands lightly over each other's body, kissing, fondling, caressing.

"The grass is dry," ventured Michael.

Emily laughed. "I didn't want to be the first to suggest sitting down."

They sat. Then, presently, they lay—not seeing each other, but hearing and touching.

"Darling Emily. I want to make love to you ... I suppose I always want to. But tonight I want it more than ever ... Do you mind? Is it—is it inconvenient?"

Again she laughed, softly. "Inconvenient! I love you, Michael. Is that inconvenient?"

"Yes, dreadfully. We are pets in a box, animals in a zoo, my dearest. We can't afford to love. It makes us vulnerable."

"Hush! It's dark, but I know there are wrinkles on your forehead, and a sad look in your eyes and your lips are tight ... We can't afford not to love, Michael. That's the truth."

"Perhaps you are right."

She shivered. "Then love me! Love me as if it were the first time and the last time."

Michael struggled with buttons and hooks. Artlessly, Emily helped him. Clothes rustled in the darkness. Then there was silence.

"You can't see me," whispered Emily. "But I'm wearing nothing at all. It's so warm, but I'm shivering and shaking—only because you touch me."

126

Michael put out a hand, and found the curve of her neck. "I can see you," he murmured. "Oh, my darling, I can see you!"

He lay on her, and Emily's legs slowly, luxuriously opened.

Like petals, thought Michael crazily. Like petals. A beautiful white flower in the darkness. And there is nectar between the petals, and I wish one could love like this and then die. And I wish ...

Emily sighed and groaned, and the petals yielded more than nectar. They yielded fire.

The lovemaking surged inexorably to a mutual climax, while both of them said and did things they did not know they were saying and doing. Afterwards, they lay close, still trying to touch each other with hands, arms, legs, breasts, faces, hair. Desire had abated, but passion had not.

Suddenly, Michael felt immensely sad; and because they were so close, the sadness instantly communicated.

"What is it, my love?" Her voice was deep now, rich with fulfilment.

And that changed his sadness into physical pain.

"Soon," said Michael, "I think you may learn to hate me."

She sat up. "What for? Whatever for? I love you, that's all."

"Darling," he said harshly, "believe that I love you, too. Dearly, lastingly. Perhaps it would be possible to leave it like this ... But, I'm going to blow up the world. I'm going to pull down the decorations, tear away the back-cloth, walk through the mirror. I'm going to get to the other side, find the real world, face it, take it for what it is ... Oh, darling, don't you see. I love you, and yet I'm a bomb. I'm going to blow us all to glory."

She began to stroke his hair, cradling his head against her breast. "You will do what is best. That's all. I know you will ... Just let us be together—even if we have to exchange *The Man In The Iron Mask* and Sunday afternoon walks in the park for a world where there are lizards and rocks and oceans and strange horizons. Just let us be together. That is enough."

Michael's face was wet. "Maybe I am not a bomb," he whispered. "Maybe I only have a talent for inspiring mass suicide."

TWENTY-FIVE

It was Ernest who arranged for Michael to meet the self-styled leader of the students of North London high school, a drybone called Arthur Wellesley. The meeting had tragic consequences which ultimately forced Michael into a course of action he had not intended.

Ernest and Jane, though their relationship was not as intense as that of Michael and Emily, had become fond of each other and had begun to spend a considerable amount of their free time together. One fine Saturday, they decided to picnic on Hampstead Heath. It was not entirely a leisure project, because Ernest was still working on his map of London and intended to draw in the more important roads in the Hampstead district.

It was while he and Jane were resting after a light lunch that they were approached by Arthur Wellesley and two other drybones whom he referred to as his lieutenants.

Arthur Wellesley was tall. He wore a white shirt, a black belt, and black trousers and shoes, as did his companions. He stood with his feet astride and one hand on his belt, as did his companions. It looked like an affectation, or a regulation pose.

Ernest and Jane were sitting on the grass on the Heath, with their picnic basket open and the remains of the meal between them. Jane was frightened by the oddly formidable appearance of the drybones.

"What are you doing here?" demanded Arthur Wellesley.

"I would have thought that was obvious," retorted Ernest calmly. "Who are you?"

"Arthur Wellesley, commander of the North London high school defence unit."

"Commander of what?"

"The North London high school defence unit. You are from the Central London group, I suppose."

"Yes. My name is Ernest Rutherford, and this is Jane Austen."

"Are you organised?" Arthur Wellesley seemed to ignore Jane's existence completely.

"Organised?"

"Militarily organised."

"No."

"You have a leader?"

"Yes, we have a leader."

"Good. Bring him here tomorrow morning. I want to talk to him."

"I don't know that he will want to talk to you."

"He will," said Arthur Wellesley with confidence. "Tell him it is important—and ask him if he knows Aldous Huxley."

With that, the three drybones simultaneously turned and marched away, perfectly in step, perfectly in line, as if they had been practising a long time.

The picnic atmosphere had evaporated, the lazy afternoon with Jane had disintegrated. Now, Ernest would have to get back as soon as possible and talk things over with Michael.

Jane was pale and shaking. Ernest put his arms round her, trying to comfort her. He realised with comical amazement then that he had never held Jane in his arms before. He had been absorbed by other matters. Too absorbed.

"They looked dangerous," explained Jane. "I—I felt they were dangerous."

"Perhaps it is because they dress the same. It's like a uniform."

"Do you think they are dangerous?"

"I don't know. Let us go and talk to Michael. That is the most intelligent thing to do."

Jane began to pack the picnic basket. "I feel cold."

"It's a warm day."

"I still feel cold. I was all right until they came ... Do you think they know about Aldous Huxley?"

Ernest shrugged. "I haven't the faintest idea. We are all taking part in what is either a nasty comedy or a funny horror film. The point is, we have to live with it, Jane. If we worry too much—if we even think about it too much—we shall go out of our minds. So just try to take things as they come, my dear. A platitude, I know. But it is the only comfort I can offer."

Jane had packed the basket, and they were ready to go.

As if on cue, an air raid began. Aeroplanes began to manoeuvre like tiny, metallic insects high in the blue sky. There was the distant crump of explosions, the chatter of guns.

Ernest looked up and began to laugh. "The war that doesn't exist. The bombs that never fall. The planes that are whisked into the fourth dimension. It is all part of the horrible comedy, the amusing nightmare ... You know Michael has read all about the real war. He told me that there was no such thing as a force field, and that half London was razed to the ground ... This doesn't even look real any more. It was good enough to fool us when we were children, but not now. Somehow, that comforts me. Perhaps the drybones are not as clever as we suspect."

Jane held herself against him. "I'm so cold," she whispered. "Deep inside I am so terribly cold."

Ernest said nothing. He held her tightly for a while. Then he tilted her face up and looked at it as if he had never seen it before. Then he kissed her—for the first and last time in their lives.

TWENTY-SIX

Michael had a fairly sleepless night. He was trying to decide whether or not it was a good thing to go to Hampstead and talk to Arthur Wellesley. When morning came he was no wiser—except that he knew that he would go.

Ernest's description of the three drybone students had not been encouraging. Even at their best, drybones were antiseptic and devious. These, according to Ernest, were also sinister; and certainly they had had a profound effect upon Jane.

There were two mysteries. Why was a drybone and not a fragile the leader of what was grandly described as the North London high school defence unit? And what, if anything, did he know of the fate of Aldous Huxley? There was only one way to find out.

Michael came down to breakfast early, expecting—since it was Sunday and Mother and Father usually slept late—to have to prepare it himself. But when he opened the dining room door he saw that the table was laid and that breakfast was almost ready.

Ever since the night they had been to see *Gone With The Wind*, Michael's relationship with his parents had deteriorated steadily. In some ways he had lost his fear of them. In other ways he had become more afraid.

"I suppose you'll be going out again today," said Father.

"Yes."

"Does it occur to you that Mother and I might like a little more of your company? We are not getting any younger."

Michael laughed harshly. "And you are not getting any older, are you? Don't waste time making speeches that sound like lines from old films, Father. It may amuse you to pretend that we are all normal people living in a normal world; but to me the joke isn't funny. It never was."

"Would you like one egg or two?" Mother's voice sounded anxious. It always did these days. She was giving a moderate to mediocre interpretation of the archetypal anxious mother, worrying about her delinquent son.

"Two, please. And lots of toast."

"Where are you going, then?" Father's voice had just the right note of indifferent curiosity.

"Just out."

"Can't you give me an intelligent answer?"

"I learned how to give unintelligent answers from you."

"You are not too old to be thrashed, you know."

"True. But I am too old to be impressed by it."

Breakfast proceeded in silence.

At the end of it, Father said surprisingly: "You can take my bicycle, if you want to. I expect you know how to ride it."

For a moment or two, Michael was dumbfounded. It was the first time Father had ever made the offer. Then he recovered himself sufficiently to say: "Thank you. I'll take care of it."

He left the house, feeling anxious and puzzled. Father might have known that Michael had quite a long journey ahead of him. But how could he possibly have known?

Michael had arranged to rendezvous with Ernest and Horatio at Hyde Park Corner. One bicycle would not be a great deal of use between the three of them; but, in taking turns on it, they could perhaps keep up a slightly faster pace than if they were all walking.

Ernest and Horatio were already at Hyde Park Corner, waiting for him.

I really must learn to expect the unexpected, he told himself grimly when he saw them. They, too, had bicycles.

"Don't tell me," he said. "The drybones spontaneously offered to let you use their bicycles."

"They are playing games with us," said Ernest despondently.

"They always have been. You know that. You should be used to it."

Horatio grinned wolfishly. "I had my favourite dream again last night. I was killing drybones with my bare hands. You know how it is in dreams. I was immensely strong, and they had become weak and brittle."

"Do what you like in dreams, Horatio," said Michael. "But remember that I meant what I said. The Aldous Huxley saga is evidently not yet finished ... Well, let's get to Hampstead and find out what new wonders there are to confound us."

Arthur Wellesley and his lieutenants were at the rendezvous, waiting. Each of them stood with feet astride and one hand on his belt. They looked like mass-produced statues, thought Michael as he wheeled his bicycle over the dewy grass, or like dancers waiting for the signal that would galvanise them into activity. Or like soldiers standing at ease.

"Rather smart," said Horatio, obviously impressed.

"Rather sinister," amended Ernest. "I suppose they mean to be."

Michael stopped a little way from the group. "Let's leave our bicycles here. And let's hope there isn't going to be any trouble."

They laid the bicycles down and walked forward. The drybones waited unmoving.

Michael said: "Hello. I'm Michael Faraday. I understand you want to talk to me."

Arthur Wellesley brought his feet together and saluted. "Wellesley, commander of the North London high school defence unit. Yes, I want to talk to you. We shall need to support each other when the revolution starts. Do you have any arms?"

Michael was shaken. "The revolution? What revolution?"

"Let's not waste words," snapped Arthur Wellesley. "I have a good intelligence service. You think the struggle is between yourselves—the people you call fragiles—and the drybones, including us. That is incorrect thinking. The true struggle is between the revolutionary and the orthodox, between the young and the old—irrespective of whether they are fragiles or drybones. Do you have any arms?"

Michael smiled faintly. "We are not planning a revolution."

"What are you planning?"

"Nothing—yet."

Arthur Wellesley laughed. "Then you will be destroyed. It is as simple as that. Unless you join forces with us."

Michael was silent for a moment or two. Then he said:

"Are there any fragiles at North London high school? I understood that—"

"There were," interrupted the drybone. "Altogether there were forty-seven."

"What happened to them?"

"They disappeared. They disappeared overnight. Whisked away without trace."

Ernest spoke. "Did you try to find out where they had gone?"

Arthur Wellesley looked him up and down, then turned to Michael. "Does this person hold any rank?"

"He is on my General Staff," said Michael gravely.

"Yes, we did try to find out where they had gone. Met with a blank wall. Nobody would discuss the matter— parents, teachers, no one. It was as if they had never existed. That is why we think you people may be in danger. That is why we think the time has come to join forces. Interested?"

"Yes, I am interested—but not wholly convinced."

"Don't wait too long to be convinced. It could be fatal."

"Yesterday, you mentioned somebody called Aldous Huxley," said Michael. "Are we supposed to know him?"

"I know that you know him. He established contact with you in the Strand Coffee House some time ago. His duty was to keep me informed of your activities. He was one of my best agents."

Horatio turned white and began to stare at the ground. Michael was afraid he might say something, or do something stupid.

"*Was* one of your best agents?"

"Yes. Was. He hasn't reported for some time ... I think he discovered something important, and I think he was liquidated. This is not a game we are playing, you know. There is no time to waste. Come along with me, and I'll show you something that will convince you we mean business. You had better bring those bicycles."

Michael and Ernest and Horatio were taken to a small suburban house in Hampstead Village. They passed a few drybones on the way; but no one paid any attention to them or to the three uniformed drybones. It was as if the occupants of Hampstead were being deliberately blind.

As they approached their destination, Arthur Wellesley's companions went through a complicated, unnecessary and absurd routine of reconnaissance to establish that they could enter the house unobserved. It was a plain little house, apparently deserted. Arthur Wellesley led the way down into the cellar and switched on the electric light.

The cellar contained racks of rifles and pistols, boxes of ammunition and grenades. There was even a light machine-gun.

Michael had never seen real lethal weapons before. He was amazed. "Where on earth did you get them?"

"An army unit was carrying out some manoeuvres on the Heath." Arthur Wellesley laughed. "So at night we carried out some manoeuvres of our own."

"I have never seen any army units in London," said Michael. "I thought they were all stationed outside the force field."

"Do you doubt my word?"

"I have no reason either to doubt it or to accept it."

"Good man! We shall get along ... About Aldous Huxley—your people didn't liquidate him, by any chance?"

"My people never liquidate anyone," said Michael carefully.

"You can't play at being damned conchies for ever," retorted Arthur Wellesley. "Otherwise you'll wind up disappearing into nowhere like our forty-seven did ... Now, what kind of arms do you need, and have you got any-where safe to keep them?"

Michael sighed. The situation was bizarre—drybones cooking up tiny dreams of revolution against drybones. But then one just had to learn to expect the unexpected. And be very, very cautious.

"Thank you for the offer—I presume it was an offer—but we are not yet ready to resort to guns, or to indulge in revolution. Not until we know exactly what we are fighting, why we are fighting and what can be gained—or lost—by fighting."

There was a brief silence.

"I see," said Arthur Wellesley. "That makes things difficult, doesn't it?"

"Why?"

"Because you know too much."

Michael smiled grimly. "On the contrary, we know too little. But I see your problem. You either have to trust us —or liquidate us."

As he spoke, Horatio stepped forward and snatched a grenade from an open box. "Any liquidation will be en-tirely democratic," he said, speaking for the first time.

Michael said: "Horatio, they won't try to kill us."

"Damn right they won't!"

Arthur Wellesley said: "You don't know how to use that thing."

Horatio grinned. "Try me. It's just like in the movies. You pull the pin and—bang."

Michael was tired, depressed, baffled. "Yes, Horatio. It's just like in the movies. Now put that thing down. We're leaving."

"No, Michael. Your way doesn't work, this time. You and Ernest get out while I keep these drybones amused. I'll join you where we left the bicycles."

Arthur Wellesley said: "You are all children, playing stupid games."

Michael ignored him. "Horatio, put it down. We'll leave together."

Horatio's voice was shrill. "Get out, both of you. I mean it. This is my affair now. And I'm going to do it my way ... Michael, you know I'm half crazy. Don't try to work out which half. Just go!"

"I think," said Ernest softly, "we had better humour him."

"I'm afraid so." Michael turned to Horatio. "All right, we'll meet at the bicycles ... Horatio, odd as it may seem, I don't think Wellesley and his friends are dangerous. Give us a minute or two then get rid of that wretched grenade and come as fast as you can."

"We shall not forget this," said Arthur Wellesley heavily.

Horatio giggled. "You may well have cause to remember it. Now kindly stand very still by the wall."

Ernest went back up the cellar steps. Michael took a last look round. It was all theatrical. So dreadfully theatrical. Horatio clutching his bomb in a roomful of bombs and ammunition, and the three drybones standing against the wall in that peculiarly formal posture with hands on belt and legs stiffly apart.

Michael wanted to say something; but there did not seem anything appropriate that he could say. He followed Ernest up the cellar steps, out of the drab little house into a grey urban Sunday.

They began to make their way quickly to where the bicycles had been left, under a covered cycle stand at the far end of the street.

They had just reached the bicycles when the explosions came. They looked back in horror and saw fragments of the house erupting into the sky. A great cloud of dust and debris seemed to hang suspended. Then the fragments of the house came crashing down.

Michael was the first to speak. "We shall never know," he said dully. "We shall never know whether Horatio intended it or whether the drybones . . ." He didn't finish.

"What do we do now?" whispered Ernest. "I suppose Horatio must be—"

"Of course he's dead!" said Michael harshly. "There is nothing to do, except get away from here as fast as we can."

TWENTY-SEVEN

Jane Austen was a very gentle person. She always had been. Gentle and timid, easily depressed, needing only simple things to make her contented—simple, unobtainable things like stability and security; but then Michael began to discover terrible secrets, and then the library yielded further terrible secrets, and now Horatio was dead. Life, which had only seemed originally like an unreal dream, was now transformed into a real nightmare. Jane Austen was living in a small claustrophobic world enclosed in a greater unknown world—reports of which only served to increase her terror and sense of impending doom. She concealed as much of her fears as possible from Ernest and Michael, realising that they must not be diverted by feminine weakness from the course they had chosen. But Emily became her confidante. Emily was a person she could trust with secrets, a person to whom she could reveal the depth of her unhappiness.

Ever since that first visit to the library, she and Emily

had spent a great deal of time in each other's company. There was little alternative, since Michael and Ernest and Horatio had been engaged in matters about which it was best to know as little as possible.

There were other fragiles that Jane knew and liked, such as Dorothy Wordsworth, Mary Kingsley and Elizabeth Barrett, but there was none whom she felt she could wholly trust—none but Emily.

On the day after Horatio's death, when school was over, she and Emily met to walk and talk in St. James's Park. Michael had decided that no one outside the Family must know what had happened to Horatio. Let the drybones find out for themselves, if they could. But the knowledge and the secrecy, the mysteries and unforeseeable dangers were a heavy burden to bear. They had become, at last, too heavy for Jane Austen.

It was a cool, grey afternoon; and hardly anyone was in the park. Emily and Jane sat on a bench and watched a pair of ducks create rippling fantasies of reflection on the mirror-like sheet of water. Emily had with her the copy of *Wuthering Heights*. Both Michael and Ernest had helped her to grasp the principles of reading; and now she was nearly half-way through the book. Sometimes she felt a strange sense of identity with that other Emily Brontë. Sometimes, she imagined she could feel the icy wind cut her face, and sense the bleak beauty of the Yorkshire moors.

Emily was acutely aware of Jane's tension and unhappiness; and had been trying to distract her with an account of the stormy adventures of Heathcliff and Cathy.

Jane was silent for a time. Then she said: "Jane Austen wrote novels, too, you know. Ernest has *The Concise Oxford Dictionary of English Literature* ... We are in there, Emily—you and me and Elizabeth Barrett and Dorothy

Wordsworth and ... and we are all trapped in little black marks on paper!" She began to sob.

Emily put her arms round Jane, trying to comfort her. "Darling Jane, don't be so unhappy. Personally, I am glad that there was another fragile called Emily Brontë who lived in a strange and wonderful world and could write such a beautiful book. Somehow, it gives me a sense of belonging. I feel at times almost as if I know her. I feel oddly as if we have something to share."

Jane stopped crying. "We have something to share, too," she said dully. "Deceit, fear, death, uncertainty. We are like little animals, Emily. Little defenceless animals in a big cage. Someone is keeping us here for a purpose, and when the purpose is fulfilled, the animals will be destroyed and the cage will be discarded."

"Michael has found a way out," said Emily.

"A way out of one nightmare and into another. Perhaps he would have done better to have left us in ignorance. Now we know that London is a—a paper city. And we also know that outside it is a world of monsters ... I—I wish we were children again, Emily. I wish that we could turn back the clock and accept what we have, and pretend that everything is all right. And everything can be all right if you pretend that it is. It *can* be."

Emily shook her head. "Not for us, Jane dear. Not in a world of fragiles and drybones. It never could have been all right. You know that."

Jane relapsed into silence once more, holding Emily's hand tightly. Presently she said: "You and Michael have made love together, haven't you?"

"Yes."

"Tell me about it. Tell me about making love. I want to know what it is like."

"It is very hard to describe, but I'll do my best. The

touching and the kissing and the stroking and the holding make my body excited, soft and hard at the same time. My breasts begin to ache and hurt, but it is the kind of ache that I don't want to stop ... When we last made love, Michael and I wore nothing at all. He lay on top of me, and my legs seemed to open without my having to think about it. And there was a hard part of him that was pressed between them, and then it went inside me. I could feel the hardness; and there was the sweetest, most consuming pain in the world ... I'm sorry. I don't know what happened really. It's funny. I don't know what making love is, or what it means, but I somehow know how to do it ... Believe this, Jane. It is the loveliest thing in the world."

"Thank you, Emily. Thank you for telling me. I still don't know what it is like. But I believe that it must be wonderful ... Do you think the drybones make love?"

Emily frowned. "I don't think the drybones even know about love. Perhaps that is something, at least, in which we are superior."

"I think I love Ernest."

Emily squeezed her hand. "I know you do. I have seen the way you look at him."

"Do you think he knows?"

"He's not as clever as he thinks he is if he doesn't ... Do you feel a bit happier now, Jane?"

"I don't know ... I feel more at peace ... Do you believe that people should have the right to decide what to do with themselves, with their lives?"

"We should all be free to make our own decisions. I suppose that, apart from finding out what our true situation is, that is what Michael and Ernest are working for."

"I don't think Horatio was working for anything like that. He just hated drybones ... I must go now, Emily.

145

My—*they* will be asking questions if I am late. I hate the questions. I hate the—the pressure."

"I must rush, too. I want to try to get out to meet Michael for a few minutes tonight. See you tomorrow, Jane. Try not to be too unhappy ... When I go to bed, I always try to fall asleep thinking of nice things. It is something I have done since I was a child."

"Yes," said Jane, standing up. "It is a good idea to fall asleep thinking of nice things ... If you see Ernest before I do tomorrow, will you do something for me?"

"Of course."

"Will you kiss him for me, and tell him that I shall love him all my life?"

Emily looked at her curiously. "Surely you would rather tell him yourself."

Jane gave a little laugh. "I don't know. Perhaps I'm too shy. Promise you will do it, Emily."

"All right. I promise."

"Thank you." Jane kissed her on the cheek, and then on the lips. "The last one," she said lightly, "is the one for Ernest." She looked at the stretch of water and sighed. "Wouldn't it be nice if we could just be silly, empty-headed ducks, dabbling in calm water for ever?"

Then she turned and walked quickly away.

Late that evening, Jane Austen took a bath. She plugged the electric radiator into the wall socket, then balanced the radiator on the end of her bath with a loop of flex hanging over. She ran the water, took off her clothes and stepped into the bath. Then she lay back, closed her eyes and thought of lovely things. After a time, still with her eyes closed, she lifted one foot out of the water and felt for the loop of flex. Then she hooked her toes behind it and jerked suddenly. The radiator fell into the water.

TWENTY-EIGHT

Michael said: "I didn't really expect you to be here tonight ... I only came for the walk. I couldn't stand watching those drybones pretending to be people ... How are you? How are you feeling, Ernest?"

"Don't worry about me," said Ernest sombrely. "The weeping is done inside. Maybe there will be a time for real tears. But not now."

It was dark, and they were standing on Waterloo Bridge; and the Thames murmured softly beneath them.

"I wish—I wish she had told us," said Michael. "I wish she had told Emily."

Ernest gave a faint smile. "Maybe she had been telling us for some time—only we didn't understand the language. And if we had understood, would we have had the right to stop her?"

"Not to stop her, perhaps, but to persuade her."

Ernest shook his head. "Pressure. Emotional blackmail.

Not on ... Jane was right to say nothing. To preserve the liberty of the individual."

"Ernest," Michael put an arm on his shoulder, "there are times when you make me feel very small."

"There are times when I make myself feel very small. This is one ... Well, Michael, the pressure mounts, the tension mounts, the tragedies begin. We know too much, and we know too little. We know that Michael Faraday and Ernest Rutherford were scientists, that Horatio Nelson was a sea captain, that Emily Brontë and Jane Austen wrote novels. We know that drybones have detachable heads and that lizards disport themselves by the sea outside London. We know that we who are called Michael Faraday, Ernest Rutherford and Emily Brontë are alive, because we feel pain. We do not know how we came to be alive or why we remain alive. We do not know if this fake city has anything at all to do with that greater, imaginary world in which we have the effrontery to believe ... So, shall we be cowards and do nothing, or shall we be cowards and do something? You are still the leader of our diminishing band. It is still you who must make the decisions."

Michael let out a great sigh. "Ernest, don't you think I have already made a mess of things?"

"Things *were* a mess. You, at least, have made us try to perceive the mess as a pattern. Whether we succeed or not, the effort is worthwhile."

"I don't like that telling phrase: diminishing band. Now, as far as we know, there are only three of us who know about the land outside London. But it is just possible that some of the other fragiles—people like Charles Darwin or Bertrand Russell or James Watt—might have been doing some independent exploration. If so, they might know things that we do not."

"I do not recall that Darwin, Russell or Watt were among those who wished to learn to read," observed Ernest dryly.

"No, but that does not preclude them from being curious in other ways ... However, whether they have used their heads or not is irrelevant. What does matter is that there are only three of *us* now. Suppose some other disasters happen—one or two could be left with the knowledge we have gained. Perhaps only Emily. What a dreadful burden that would be."

"Then what do you propose?"

"An end to secrecy, an end to deception. An end to the double-thinking that compels us to behave with apparent normality in this grotesquely abnormal situation."

"You may also be proposing an end to living."

"That is the risk, but it is a risk we have to take ... Ernest, let us suppose the existence of some mad scientist —just as in one of those terrible children's films they expect us to watch. Let us endow this scientist with almost unlimited means, so that, for the purpose of his work, he is able to create this illusory London—and even, perhaps, able to create us."

"Now we are really taking off into the realms of fancy," commented Ernest dryly.

"We never left them," retorted Michael. "What I am getting at is this: so long as we fragiles are unconscious or compliant victims, the experiment—or whatever it is —can proceed. But what happens if all the guinea pigs know they are being used. What happens if they all begin to investigate the aims of the scientist?"

"The experiment is terminated," said Ernest. "The guinea pigs are destroyed ... Or set free ... But we know nothing, Michael. We have only acquired a collection of mysteries. For all we know, we may not even be on Earth."

Michael was silent for a time. Then he said: "I am convinced of one thing. Behind the apparent unreason there is reason." He held out his arms in a gesture that seemed to encompass the whole of London. "It is just too much to believe that all this—ourselves included—was created for some idiotic caprice. There must be a purpose ... Do you remember that day, long ago—it's hard to imagine how long ago—when we were in play school and Miss Shelley told us about the Overman legend?"

"I do." Ernest was excited. "The odd thing is, nobody has mentioned it since."

"Once," said Michael. "Once Father mentioned it. After we had been to see *Gone With the Wind*. There was a quarrel because I had been asking too many questions. In the end, he told me to ask myself if any of the Overman legend could be true ... I remember something else, too. Suddenly, I remember something else. That night, after Miss Shelley had told us the story, Father asked me what I thought of it. But I hadn't mentioned anything about it. So how could he have known?"

"Therefore he knew beforehand."

"Therefore," said Michael, "it is probably significant. How about someone or something called Overman for the mad scientist? For some reason I can't understand, the end of the story comes into my mind. Overman says: The problem is this. Shall men control machines or shall machines control men? Then there is something about going to sleep for ten thousand years."

"Fantasies," sighed Ernest. "Fantasies. Eventually we shall go mad."

"No, Ernest. We may be destroyed—but destruction

is better than madness. Tomorrow is the last time we shall ever attend that idiotic school. Tomorrow is the last time we shall ever do anything the drybones want us to do."

Ernest gave a bitter laugh. "The revolt of the guinea pigs. I like it. But is it to be just two guinea pigs—or three?"

"As many as are tired of living in a cage. We must get all the fragiles together, somehow, and tell them what we know. Away from school. But how can we do that?"

Ernest thought for a moment or two. "I suppose we could say it was a matter of life and death, and swear them to secrecy."

"Secrecy! There's little chance of that."

"Which may be a good thing," said Ernest surprisingly. "After all, we want an end to secrecy, for ever ... Why don't we ask every one to rendezvous in Hyde Park by the old play school? It's easy enough for us all to get to."

"It is as good a place as any. In fact, it is singularly appropriate. Play school! We have been living in one all our lives ... Oh, well, let's go home, Ernest, and go to bed for the last time like clockwork people. I must think what I am going to say tomorrow—assuming anybody turns up."

"Some will come," said Ernest. "Sheer curiosity ... Michael, I wonder what happened to the fragiles at North London high school? Perhaps they tried something like this."

Michael sighed. "I think there never were any fragiles at North London high school—if, indeed, there is a North London high school. It was just part of the experiment. That's all."

He looked up at the sky. The clouds were thinning out

and patterns of stars were beginning to appear. I wonder, he thought, if those are the patterns one should be able to see over a city called London on a planet called Earth.

TWENTY-NINE

Play school was derelict—an empty house with no function. A shell with convolvulus and ivy climbing up the walls. A mausoleum of childhood. A memento mori.

Michael sat on the garden wall near the gate. He was alone. Emily and Ernest were busy—he hoped—persuading the other fragiles to come and hear the oracle speak.

Michael was alone; alone and cold in the late afternoon sunlight. Alone with bizarre thoughts, and memories that offered no comfort. Several times he had silently counted the number of fragiles that he knew. There were only forty-three. No matter how hard he tried, he could not make the number any larger. His mind had been playing tricks. He had imagined there would be more—considerably more.

Forty-three fragiles in the whole of London! Then how many drybones? Five hundred, a thousand, two thousand? Impossible to estimate. But the drybones had been sufficient for their purpose. There had been enough of them to convince—for a time, at least.

Michael shivered. The air was warm; but thoughts and feelings were bitterly cold. Sitting on the wall, he remembered the time when all the children at play school had been sent on an adventure walk to collect leaves. He remembered the little girl who had followed him, the girl with yellow hair who was called Ellen Terry. He remembered how he had tried to lose her; how he had tried to outpace her; how, in desperation, he had at last tried to kill her. But he had discovered that drybones don't die easily.

And he remembered about the odd little boy who screamed that he hated children because they were not real people, because they could not take off their heads. The little boy who was carried screaming and kicking out of the room, and was never seen again. And Michael remembered how little Horatio Nelson had calmly advised him that if he wished to kill Ellen Terry he would have to push her out of a high window.

Poor Horatio. He had learned to hate and fear drybones before anyone else had ...

Michael looked up and saw that a few groups of people were strolling across Hyde Park towards play school. Judging by the numbers, Emily and Ernest must have been far more successful than he had dared hope. Suddenly, he began to feel optimistic. But his optimism was short-lived. The figures were revealed not as fragiles but as drybones, all of them. More groups were following. They came towards Michael and stood a few paces away from him in a semi-circle, silent, waiting.

They gazed at him, expressionless. Cold sweat began to trickle in rivulets down his face. The semi-circle grew and grew. It seemed to contain almost every drybone that Michael had ever seen or known. There were his own parents, parents of other fragiles, teachers, drybones who were familiar background figures in streets and parks. There was Aldous Huxley—except that it couldn't be Aldous Huxley, because Aldous Huxley was dead. And there was Arthur Wellesley—except that it couldn't be Arthur Wellesley ...

They all gazed at him in silence. Michael was shaking with fear. He wanted to run, scream, die. But pride made him stay seated on the wall. He wiped the sweat from his eyebrows, and hoped that the drybones did not know that he was half paralyzed with fear.

The waiting, the silent waiting seemed to expand into an eternity. But presently, other, smaller groups came across the park—the fragiles, at last. Michael was too numb to try to count them; but it looked as if most had come. They, too, were amazed at the presence of so many drybones, and stood for a while at the perimeter of the crowd, gazing anxiously at Michael.

Then Emily slowly worked her way through the crowd and came to the front. So did Ernest. So did one or two more fragiles. Their nearness cheered Michael a little, and strengthened him. Emily smiled and her smile somehow began to melt the freezing paralysis.

Michael stood up on the wall. As he did so, Queen Victoria's hovercar came gliding swiftly across the park. It stopped close to the edge of the crowd. Out stepped Sir Winston Churchill, who then turned and gave his arm to support the Queen.

"Well, young jackanapes," called Sir Winston in a surprisingly loud voice, "I hear you think you are important enough to babble some nonsense or other to the good citizens of London. Out with it, boy, then we can all have a laugh and go home to our tea. And mark democracy in

155

action, boy. Even the Queen is prepared to listen to your blather—at least, for a time."

"Sir Winston," said the Queen, "pray do not be too hard upon the young man. Freedom of speech is one of the values for which we have waged a just and terrible war for so long."

Michael stared at them. At last he understood. The pattern was to be intimidation and ridicule. He was to be discredited and humiliated in front of the other fragiles. That was how the truth would be destroyed.

He looked at Emily and Ernest. Their faces were white, drawn. But suddenly, Michael himself was no longer afraid. It was as if fear was a dark tunnel; and, miraculously, he had just come out at the other end into sanity and daylight.

"Your Majesty, Sir Winston," said Michael calmly, "since you are not here by invitation, perhaps you would be good enough to remain silent. What I have to say is meant for my friends."

Gasps and murmurs came from the crowd.

"Ho, ho!" roared Sir Winston. "The boy has spirit. He also claims to have friends. Where are they?"

"Here are two." It was Ernest's voice. He took Emily by the hand and led her to the play school wall to stand near Michael.

"Michael, come here. You are making a fool of yourself." That was Father's voice.

"That is the point!" shouted Michael. "It is you and all the other mechanical imitations of people who have been trying to make fools of us. You, the drybones, the ones who don't bleed. You have tried to keep us as children, you have tried to destroy our independence of thought."

"Your Majesty," roared Sir Winston, "I greatly fear this is treason."

"You are right, Sir Winston," snapped Michael, "it is treason. I am rebelling against imprisonment, I am rebelling against tyranny of the mind, I am rebelling against a collection of machines with interchangeable faces. Above all, I am rebelling against my own ignorance and your deliberate deception. And eventually I am leaving this toy city you call London. And if you stop me, or if I disappear, all my friends—all the true people, the ones who can bleed—will know what has happened. And if that occurs, your own plans will come to nothing ... There are not many of us. You could easily destroy us all. But you will not do that because, if you did, you would be left without purpose and with nothing but useless machinery."

"Sir Winston," said the Queen angrily, "I will hear no more of this—this abuse. Let us leave the madman, and I recommend all honest citizens to do likewise."

"Scoundrel," shouted Sir Winston, "you will live to regret this. I shall advise the Queen to recall the Brigade of Guards."

"Advise her also," said Michael, "to stay out of my way. Advise all drybones to stay out of *our* way. We have had enough."

Sir Winston helped Queen Victoria into her hovercar. Then he got in after her. The hovercar sped smoothly away.

"Michael Faraday, I disown you!" That was Father's voice again. "The Queen is right, as always. All sensible people will leave this place. Only traitors will remain."

"Go and choke on your own clichés," said Michael evenly. "Your task is over. If it was to make me grow up to accept this nonsensical world, you failed badly."

In twos and threes, the drybones began to drift away, some murmuring, some making threatening gestures that now seemed oddly comical. Michael wondered with amazement now why he had been so dreadfully afraid. Then suddenly he understood. It was a joke—a rich, rich joke. It was not the fragiles but the machines who had been on a no-win basis. Their experiment—or whatever it was—contained its own defeat. If the machines restrained the fragiles, it failed. If the machines did not restrain the fragiles, it failed. It could only ever have succeeded if the fragiles had remained passive, uncurious, unadventurous.

Michael looked at those who remained, and counted them. Forty-two fragiles—and himself.

They looked at him, some amazed, some bewildered, some smiling, some proud.

He felt a great surge of kinship. These, he thought, are my brothers, my sisters. I belong to them, and they to me. From now on, the fantasy, the pretence, is over. From now on, what we do, we will do together, and we will do it openly. We will never submit to the drybones again.

He climbed down from the wall and held Emily's hand. The other fragiles came closer. Charles Darwin, Mary Kingsley, Dorothy Wordsworth, Joseph Lister, James Watt, Charles Babbage, Elizabeth Barrett, John Dalton ...

"Now," said Michael, "we are the only real people in this place we have been taught to call London. At last we can all speak freely and openly to each other. I think there is a great deal to be said and a great deal to be decided. Whatever happens, life can never be the same for us again."

THIRTY

The fragiles talked to each other. At last someone had
had the courage to confront the drybones with secret
and forbidden thoughts and—most important of all—to
defy the drybones, to challenge their aims and actions,
their authority. At last the psychological barriers were
down, and the fragiles felt free to talk to each other as
they had never talked before.

For a time, there was babbling chaos as people crowded
around Michael, asking questions, contributing their own
items of information. For a time, they could not stop
speaking, chattering, even laughing. Until now they had
not realised the depths of their inhibitions, the extent
of the loneliness and mistrust and insecurity to which
they had been driven by the drybones.

Amid the torrent of words, Michael discovered that
others had begun a programme of exploration. James Watt
had already discovered that the Thames was not a river.

Charles Darwin had found that there were no roads leading out of the city.

At length, when the first dizzy exhilaration of freedom had subsided a little, Ernest was able to call the fragiles to order so that Michael could now carry out his original intention of making public all that had been discovered so far.

Few of the fragiles were greatly surprised to learn about the Thames or the roads; but they were all immensely excited to learn of the existence of the library and its contents. Those who had long ago joined in the laughter and ridicule when Michael and Ernest had persisted in their determination to read now bitterly regretted their own lack of confidence and interest, the subtle conditioning of the drybones.

Michael explained how he had discovered that the war was a farce, that in reality it had been an entirely different war, and that—according to the books—it was now part of history. He also told of the discovery that every fragile, or almost every fragile, had names that were the same as great writers, scientists, explorers. And he recounted the exploration of one of the underground passages leading from the library, the destruction of Aldous Huxley, the discovery of his body in the strange world that lay outside London. Finally, he explained how Horatio Nelson had died and how Jane Austen's suicide had convinced him that there could no longer be any secrecy; there could no longer be any division among the fragiles.

"It comes finally to this," said Michael, gazing at faces he was learning to see anew, at people he was learning to love and accept and respect, "we are the true human beings, the *real* ones ... There are very few of us—why, I do not know. But I am sure we will find out." He extended his arms in a dramatic gesture. "All this—this elaborate stage scenery was, I am sure, constructed entirely for us. We, therefore, are the precious ones. *They* are expendable. *They* are only instruments designed for a purpose. And the purpose lies with us."

"What shall we do now?" asked Mary Kingsley.

"Find out as much as we can as fast as we can," answered Michael. "The great deception is over. The dry-bones know it is over. So we no longer have to explore by stealth. From now on, we do whatever we need to do openly. I suggest that we go to Apollo Twelve Square, to the London Library. Horatio found two underground passageways. So far, we have only been able to explore one. I suggest that we split ourselves into three groups: one to hold the library against any—any intrusion, and the other groups to explore both passageways ... Eventually—if we remain here long enough—we will set up reading lessons so that everyone can discover for himself what lies in the books."

"How do we know the books were not manufactured by the drybones?" asked Joseph Lister. "Like they have manufactured everything else for us."

"We don't know," said Michael. "You will have to judge for yourself. But it seems to me that the books in London Library contain thoughts and ideas and knowledge beyond anything ever experienced or hinted at by any drybone we know ... Those books *smell* of people —real people. I'm sure you will find—as I found—an awareness of truth, a desire to communicate ... Truth is what the drybones have always denied us. You will recognise it instantly when you see it. Like a hungry man recognising food."

"If we are going to the library," said Ernest, "I think it would be unwise to lose any more time. The drybone mind is inscrutable. They obviously provided the books;

and it might just occur to them that they could slow us down by taking the books away."

Michael was suddenly anxious. That would be an obvious drybone retaliation. But perhaps too obvious. These days, the drybones were being more subtle than formerly. Nevertheless, the fragiles could not now afford to risk losing their precious store of books.

"Ernest is right. We must get to Apollo Twelve Square as fast as we can. I should have thought of that before."

Emily squeezed his hand. "It is going to be all right. I have an odd feeling that the drybones are not going to obstruct us any more."

THIRTY-ONE

London Library looked desolate and deserted, just as it was when Michael had first seen it. The boards that had once been across the doorway lay where Horatio had dropped them when he had prized them away. The windows were as grimy as ever. The door was not locked.

But the library was not entirely deserted.

When Michael stepped inside he saw that someone was standing in the centre of the room, an open book in his hand, reading aloud.

It was Mr. Shakespeare.

As the rest of the fragiles filed into the library, they heard Mr. Shakespeare's quiet voice:

"In some way the material universe appears to be passing away like a tale that is told, dissolving into nothingness like a vision. The human race, whose intelligence dates back only a single tick of the astronomical clock, could hardly hope to understand so soon what it all means.

Some day perhaps we shall know: at present we can only wonder."

When Michael had first encountered Mr. Shakespeare as the head of high school, he had not been able to decide whether he was a fragile or a drybone. With his white hair and wrinkled face, Mr. Shakespeare looked very old —and very human. Even now, Michael was not entirely sure.

Mr. Shakespeare closed the book and put it down. *"The Stars In Their Courses,"* he said. "Sir James Jeans. A most interesting book. You must read it some time ... Well, Michael, I expected you sooner. But I expect there was some discussion."

"Yes," said Michael, "there was some discussion ... I hope you are not here to obstruct us."

Mr. Shakespeare smiled benignly, and shook his head. "Improbable as it may seen, I am here to inform and assist. I do not expect you to trust me. I shall be content if you accept my services."

"Are you—?" began Michael. He stopped, confused.

"No, Michael, I cannot bleed. I am a drybone, like the others."

"Then why are you offering to help us?" asked Ernest.

Mr. Shakespeare laughed. "Ernest, you have always demonstrated exceptional intelligence. Can you not think of a reason?"

Ernest was silent for a moment or two. Then he said: "So Michael was right. Now that the guinea pigs have rebelled, the experiment is really over."

"Hardly. In a sense, the experiment is about to begin. But I will not confuse you any more. The time for confusion is past. The time for understanding—for total understanding—begins."

"We came here to explore two passageways," said
164

Michael. "It has just occurred to me that you may be trying to divert us until other drybones get here."

Mr. Shakespeare sighed. It seemed a very human kind of sigh. "You are right to be suspicious, Michael. You have conditioned yourself to suspect the motives of dry-bones for a long time. If you wish to carry out your explorations immediately, do so. I will do nothing at all to hinder you. But I think you would be more psychologically prepared if you were to listen first to what I have to say."

Michael considered for a moment or two. "We will give you a little time," he said at last. "But if your information is the kind of information we have been given in the past, we will destroy you."

"I can guarantee that it is not."

"Then give us facts that mean something."

"Certainly. But there is a lot to be assimilated, Michael. And it must be taken slowly. First, the city of London and we drybones were created entirely to serve you—and to test you."

"Why to test us?"

"Because it was necessary to know what human beings are like—what levels of intelligence they can attain, how they react in adversity, how they can be intellectually frustrated or stimulated, what motivates them and so on."

"If it was necessary to find out what human beings are like," said Ernest, "then this project cannot have been mounted by human beings."

"It was not."

Michael took a deep breath. "Then we are not on the planet Earth."

"Yes, Michael, you are on the planet Earth. You are on an island—quite a pleasant island from the human point

165

of view—that was once called Tasmania. You are the only human beings on the entire planet, and you were especially developed for this project. You are the Overman culture."

Michael's throat was dry. His heart was pounding in his chest. Emily's hand lay cold in his. He dared not look at her.

"Who—or what—developed us?" Michael's voice was suddenly hoarse.

"A vast machine complex," said Mr. Shakespeare. "So vast that it will take you a long time even to begin to understand part of its functions ... A few moments ago, you talked of destroying me, Michael. This is something you cannot do. Because all drybones are merely extensions of the same thing. For example, everyone of us knew when Horatio Nelson destroyed the Huxley component. Everyone of us knew what happened when Ellen Terry followed you, as a child, to make you lose your temper. All of us knew exactly what Arthur Wellesley said on Hampstead Heath. All the time, we have all known simultaneously and instantaneously what each of us was experiencing or recording. Because I and every other drybone are one ...

"Listen to the Churchill function." Mr. Shakespeare's benevolent expression remained the same, but his voice changed radically. *"Boy, you should be home in bed. All children should be home in bed!"*

The fragiles in the library gasped in amazement. The voice was exactly that of Sir Winston Churchill; and Michael knew that the words were exactly as they had been spoken on a frosty autumn evening long ago.

"Now the Victoria function: *You want too much, child. You want far too much.*"

The Queen's voice was unmistakable.

166

"Now, the Ellen Terry function: *Poor Michael. I was only teasing.*"

Michael vividly recalled Ellen Terry's laughter as he tried to bite her throat.

Again Mr. Shakespeare spoke in his normal voice. "So you see, we are only extensions of the machine that has brought you, the Overman culture, to maturity."

Michael's own voice was unsteady. "You have not yet told us what kind of machine it is."

"Our identity is defined as Intercon Comcom Zero Nine—Intercontinental Computer Complex Nine—the last and greatest computer system in the world."

There was a brief silence. No one moved. It was as if the awesome revelations had temporarily paralysed the fragiles. Michael gazed at Mr. Shakespeare. Late sunlight slanting through the library window lent a subtle radiance to his white hair and wrinkled face. A subtle illusion of humanity rested on this component of Intercontinental Computer Complex Nine.

Michael tried to think of Mr. Shakespeare as an instrument being used by a distant machine, and thought the effort would probably cost him his sanity.

His mouth was dry. His tongue felt like parchment. Michael licked his lips and spoke with difficulty. "You called us the Overman culture. Tell us why—and tell us clearly. Above all, we have to know what we are."

"You explored only one passage, Michael. Eventually, you would have explored the other. You would have discovered for yourselves all that you need to know. But perhaps it is as well that I am here to lead the way. Come, then, and see your origins."

Mr. Shakespeare turned towards the door at the far end of the library.

THIRTY-TWO

"This is mankind!" The words seemed to come from nowhere and everywhere. They echoed and reverberated between the dark green glassy walls, the black shiny floor and the illuminated ceiling of the vast chamber.

The journey down the underground passage had not been long—nowhere near as long as down the passage that led outside London—and now the fragiles were confronted by a scene that was both terrible and wonderful.

"This is mankind!" said the voice once more. "You are now in the Overman Suspension Vault. I am Cryogenics Control, Station One. I have you on my screens. Greetings and Welcome. You are standing in the preservation chamber that was constructed for Julius Overman in the twenty-first century of the Christian era. Here lie the last three natural-born human beings on Earth."

Michael was in a state of shock, as were the other fragiles. He looked at the great chamber, at the intricate system of pipes, at the panel displaying a bewildering array of gauges and dials, and at the three large, transparent, triple-walled cylinders containing the bodies of three naked human beings—a man and two women.

"Let me explain." Mr. Shakespeare's voice was oddly gentle. "This chamber was discovered one hundred and fifty years ago. It was discovered during a magnetometric survey of the island of Tasmania. These bodies, preserved in liquid helium, are the bodies of Julius Overman and his two wives, Abigail and Mary. Until they were placed in the cylinders, none of them clinically dead. Julius Overman had his preservation chamber constructed very well by the standards of the time, with primary, secondary and tertiary circuits for all electronic and cryogenic systems. There were automated repair networks and three independent cryogenics control systems. There were heat-exchange power units designed to function in sequence for a very long time. Unfortunately, no mechanical system can function with perfect efficiency indefinitely, and no biological system can be preserved indefinitely. Mr. Overman and his wives have been in suspension too long. There is irreversible brain damage."

Michael looked at Emily. Tears were trickling unheeded from her eyes as she stared at the huge cylinders. He knew why she was crying. She was crying for the immense loneliness, the immense sadness of three human beings, caught in crystal, frozen beyond life, beyond death, locked into history, an icy epitaph for an entire civilisation.

Then he looked at Ernest, and saw the tragic understanding in his eyes. Then he looked at the other fragiles. Some were unable to bear the sight, and held each other tightly, hiding their heads against breasts or shoulders. Others stared, awed, saddened, oppressed.

At last Michael found his voice. He turned to Mr.

Shakespeare. "You say they have been in these cylinders too long. How long is too long?"

"Ten thousand years," said Mr. Shakespeare. "They entered these suspension units in the same century during which the race of man destroyed itself. Later, when you have received special training, you will be able to understand exactly what happened. But it is sufficient now for me to explain that, during the twenty-first century, there were four great military and technological powers in the world. They were the North American Federation, the United States of Europe, the Russian Commonwealth and the Sino-Japanese Republic. The first nuclear war was between the North American Federation and the Sino-Japanese Republic. It destroyed over two thousand million human beings. During the second nuclear war, which took place towards the end of the century, between the Russian Commonwealth and the United States of Europe, a doomsday weapon was eventually used. It is impossible to determine whether it was used by accident or by design. In this case the doomsday weapon consisted of a self-replicating biochemical poison, dispersed by air and water, which attacked the central nervous system of almost all primates—especially man. Climatic dispersal brought about the destruction of the entire human race within a few decades."

Michael did not clearly understand all that Mr. Shakespeare was saying, but the general pattern was clear. Clear—and horrible to imagine. Suddenly, he was struck by a thought. "This poison—is it still active? Outside ... outside London?"

"The poison was eventually neutralised, but far too late to save any human beings."

Michael's head and his entire body seemed to be aching with shock, with sadness and with a profound awe. At the same time, he felt oddly numb. He wondered if the other fragiles felt like this. He marvelled that he seemed to be still capable of rational speech.

"If the human race is dead," he said slowly, "then what are we?"

Mr. Shakespeare smiled. "You are the second human race. There is much to explain. But first, it is my duty to present to you the testament of Julius Overman."

THIRTY-THREE

Mr. Shakespeare went to the instrument panel that was fixed against the glassy walls of the vault. There were several switches and studs under the rows of dials, gauges and meters. Every switch but one was protected by a glass covering. Mr. Shakespeare pointed to the switch and to a small ceramic tile underneath it on which there appeared to be words.

"Michael, despite some discouragement and a great deal of derision, you persisted in your intention to learn to read. These instructions are in the English language. Would you care to read them?"

Michael walked across the vault to the instrument panel and looked at the tile.

"Let no man use this switch," he read, "or disturb those now sealed in this chamber, unless he truly loves his fellow men."

"I believe," said Mr. Shakespeare, "that you, Michael Faraday, are qualified to operate the device."

Michael pressed the switch.

There was a faint hissing. Then a small section of wall close to the instrument panel opened outwards to reveal a lighted recess. All it contained was a rectangular plate of metal that looked like bronze.

Michael lifted the heavy plate out of the recess. It was deeply engraved with row upon row of words. The first line Michael could read; but the second, third and fourth he could not. The fifth line he could read; but the sixth, seventh and eighth he could not. The ninth he could read; and so it went on.

Mr. Shakespeare glanced at the plate. "The other languages are French, Russian and Chinese," he said. "If translated, they would yield the same information as the English text. It is ten thousand years since human eyes have seen these words, Michael. It is now your privilege to reveal the testament of Julius Overman."

Michael held the plate firmly and read aloud.

"I, Julius Overman, new Mormon, of the Church of Jesus Christ of the Latter Day Saints, do hereby deliver this my testament to whomsoever shall find it, and my soul into the keeping of God, secure in the knowledge of eternal life.

"I was born in the year 1977 in London, England, to which corrupt and decadent country I shall not return until time and the will of God have wrought great and cleansing changes. The world is evil and is bent upon a course of great destruction. I cannot share in its evil ways nor do I wish to reap the harvest of destruction that must surely come. For I believe that mankind is determined to try the infinite patience of God; and I believe that in the end by His just and righteous anger the nations of the Earth shall perish.

"But shall mankind be utterly destroyed because of

the evil in the civilisation that exists today? God is merciful. It is not His will that the seed of Adam shall yield such a final harvest. God is merciful and has given to me, Julius Overman, lowly sinner that I am, the task of preparing for the coming of a new human race on that day when He shall cause this vault to be opened, and shall bring forth His servants into a new Eden.

"Therefore, being a person of substance in this world where wealth is mistaken for virtue, I have obeyed the instructions of my Lord. I have divested myself of all worldly possessions, and I have caused this chamber to be built in a small and yet unspoiled land far from my natural home. I have gathered genetic material on the advice of scientific men of good will, and I have caused it to be preserved here in the manner which, I believe, God has revealed to man for this very purpose. Also have I instructed my good and obedient wives Abigail and Mary in the sacred design with which my Lord has honoured me. Therefore we now resign ourselves to that sleep from which, in the fulness of time, it shall please the Almighty to awaken us.

"If it be His purpose to preserve others as we also are preserved, so that the mysteries of this chamber shall be revealed to humankind, I entreat any such persons in the Name of the Lord, to follow exactly the resuscitation procedures that are engraved in many tongues on the reverse side of this sheet of bronze.

"Now, therefore, do we, Julius, Abigail and Mary lovingly and obediently commit ourselves to the mercy of God, knowing that though the coldness of death enter our hearts and bodies, yet shall faith and love sustain our spirits joyfully until that time when evil has gone from this world, and the ways of the Lord are manifest."

Michael laid the plate carefully back in the recess, and

turned to gaze once more at the bodies in the transparent cylinders. A tumult of thoughts and sensations erupted in his mind. He tried to imagine the millennia throughout which those pathetic bodies had been preserved—and couldn't. He tried to imagine the kind of faith that would enable three people to voluntarily commit themselves to a state that was neither death nor life—and couldn't. He tried to imagine the scale of the warfare and the power of the weapons that had destroyed mankind almost ten thousand years ago—and couldn't. His imagination was overwhelmed. His comprehension was reeling.

At last Mr. Shakespeare spoke. "An attempt was made to resuscitate these people," he said quietly. "The bodies reacted with limited response. The hearts were restarted, respiration was achieved. But brain damage had reduced the minds to levels below that of idiocy. So the bodies were returned to their cylinders to be preserved until other human beings became competent to decide their future. However, the genetic material—the sperm and ova—collected by Julius Overman and preserved by the same techniques to which he submitted himself and his wives, was in excellent condition. It could be used. It was used ... Before the human race was destroyed, it was common for scientists to culture living organisms for experimental purposes. The material found in this chamber has been more than sufficient to culture or generate the nucleus of a new human race. That nucleus has been designated the Overman culture."

There was silence, but it did not last for long. One or two of the fragiles began to weep quietly, others comforted them. Elizabeth Barrett fainted. Joseph Lister and Dorothy Wordsworth looked after her, stroked her forehead, coaxed her back into consciousness.

Michael looked at Emily. She was pale and drawn, and

175

seemed to be swaying a little. He went to her, put his arms round her, gave her the reassurance of strength and of warm and living flesh.

"I don't think we can take any more, Michael," she murmured. "We need to rest, to recover from ... from ..."

"From the truth," said Michael with a faint smile. "From the terrible truth. I think it is stranger than anything we have ever suspected."

"Emily is right," said Ernest, mopping his forehead with a handkerchief. "We badly need to rest, all of us. I don't know how you feel Michael. But I feel proud, excited, saddened, awed and terrified all at once."

Mr. Shakespeare spoke once more. "May I make a suggestion? It is evident that the experience has been emotionally and intellectually exhausting for all of you. As of now, all drybones—all humanoid components, including myself—are programmed to accept all reasonable commands. It is possible to arrange transport from London Library to your homes and—"

"We are not going back to our homes," said Michael harshly. "We are not going back to pseudo-parents and reminders of a fake existence. Above all, we are not going to be separated from each other. Not now."

"Very well, Michael. What are your instructions?"

Michael thought for a moment or two. "The library is large enough for a temporary refuge—in fact it is very appropriate, for here we have the works of other fragiles, other people, to keep us company ... Can you arrange for beds and food to be brought to the library?"

Mr. Shakespeare smiled. "The operation is already beginning ... You wanted the truth, Michael. You have always wanted the truth. You have discovered some of it today. Tomorrow, I hope you will allow me to escort you to Buckingham Palace, where another aspect can be revealed."

"Why should we go to Buckingham Palace?"

"To learn something of the nature of artificial intelligence. Shall we make our way back to the library so that you may all relax? By the time we arrive, food and other comforts will have been installed."

Michael looked once more at the three motionless bodies, sealed in their transparent containers. It was ironic that the future of human life on Earth really had depended upon the convictions of a religious fanatic. Just possibly Julius Overman's faith might eventually be justified in a way he could never have foreseen or imagined.

Suddenly, a thought struck Michael. He turned to Mr. Shakespeare. "How long ago did you begin to develop the—the Overman culture? As you have confused us in other ways, you drybones have always confused our sense of time. I assume there were reasons."

"Yes, Michael, there were reasons. The experiment began almost twenty-one years ago." Mr. Shakespeare smiled at the assembled fragiles. "Ladies and gentlemen, you are all just over twenty years old."

THIRTY-FOUR

The hoverbus whined to a halt; and the fragiles—the Overman culture, the nucleus of the second human race —stepped out into the courtyard of Buckingham Palace. Michael wondered why no one had ever attempted to explore Buckingham Palace before. It was not guarded. It never had been guarded; and in retrospect it seemed an obvious target. But the conditioning given by the drybones had been good. It had been hard enough to break that conditioning to the extent of trying to explore London, and learning to read.

The night spent in the library had been harrowing, exciting and finally restful. For the first time in their lives, forty-three human beings felt both free and united. They had been made free by their discovery of the truth; and they had been united by the discovery of their origin. After they had eaten and rested, there had been a great deal of excited discussion—about Julius Overman and his fantastic project, about the sudden subservience of the drybones, and above all about the world outside London, an entire planet of which they were the natural inheritors. Eventually, fatigue put an end to the discussion. Eventually, Emily fell asleep in Michael's arms for the very first time ...

The hoverbus had been waiting for them in the morning. The ride in it, though short, was exciting. It was the first time any of the Overman culture had ridden in a motorised vehicle.

Mr. Shakespeare, bland and benevolent, escorted them to the main door of the palace. Queen Victoria herself opened it.

"Good morning," she said. "I trust you all slept well and that the shock of discovering the suspension vault did not prove too exhausting. The palace would have been at your disposal, of course, but—"

"But we preferred the society of the dead," said Michael dryly. "Now that your majesty is defined as a humanoid component of Intercontinental Computer Complex Nine, I presume we may dispense with formalities."

The Queen smiled. "Michael, you are a natural leader. Complex Nine wishes you well."

Sir Winston Churchill stepped forward. "Congratulations, my boy. Tenacity, determination, intelligence— you have them all. Have you breakfasted, now?"

"You know we have breakfasted," said Michael evenly. "You are all one."

Sir Winston chuckled and led Queen Victoria away. "They will adapt very well," he said. "Now, perhaps, they are ready to begin again."

Mr. Shakespeare spoke. "Forgive the diversions. Complex Nine has its own type of humour. If you will follow me, you will soon learn much about the nature of artificial intelligence."

He led Michael and his companions to what was, apparently, a reception hall. He led them towards its far wall. As they approached it, the wall divided in the middle and then swung back to reveal a deep chamber. It appeared to contain row upon row of large, uniformly-sized, metal-plated cabinets. Between the rows of cabinets was what looked like the track of a miniature railway. At the far end of the chamber there was a large white screen. Facing the screen and some distance away from it were three rows of chairs. Michael noticed that there was a subdued humming in the room, and a faintly antiseptic smell.

"You are now in the Tasmanian sub-station of Complex Nine," said Mr. Shakespeare. "This is the thinking machine, the artificial intelligence of which I am an extension. My physical presence is no longer necessary. But I will remain, if you wish."

"Stay with us," said Michael with a faint smile. "You, at least, are something with which we are familiar."

"From Complex Nine to the Overman culture, greetings," said a quiet voice that seemed to come from everywhere. "You have many questions; but before those questions are answered it is important that you should have some appreciation of my nature.

"You are self-conscious beings whose sense of identity is seated in the brain. I, too, am a self-conscious being, whose sense of identity lies in electronic circuitry and memory-storage units contained in this room and in other centres throughout the world. I will use my maintenance apparatus to give a simple demonstration."

A machine looking oddly like a spider on wheels rolled along the miniature railway track to one of the cabinets, removed a metal plate and took out of the cabinet a small ring, which it brought to Michael.

Michael took hold of the ring, which seemed to be made of some kind of plastic and was slightly warm.

"Encoded in the ring," said the voice, "is the basic Shakespeare programme. Observe the humanoid component that brought you here."

Everyone looked at Mr. Shakespeare. He was motionless. Ernest went to him and touched him. He fell over, hitting the floor rigidly.

The spider-like mechanism then restored the ring to its cabinet. Mr. Shakespeare picked himself up off the floor.

"Ladies and gentlemen," said the quiet voice. "It is necessary for you to understand something of the development of thinking machines. Please seat yourselves in front of the screen."

When they had done so, the voice continued.

"Electronic computers were developed by man only one hundred years before he brought about his own destruction. The first computers were simple machines, large and cumbersome. Their very operation had to be programmed by human beings. They were used to carry out tedious calculations that would otherwise have absorbed a great deal of human energy. Later, computers were used to guide military missiles, to control production lines and large industrial complexes, to plot the course of space vehicles, to analyse data and make forecasts. On the screen you will now see some of the early computers and the work they carried out."

There were shots of automated assembly lines and of the tape and disc computers used to control them. There were shots of busy offices and of computer print units turning out work that could otherwise only have been accomplished by hundreds of human clerks. There were shots of missiles lifting off, and close-ups of the guidance units they employed. There were shots of the Computer Centre at Cape Kennedy, and of the first manned journey to the moon.

All the time, the quiet voice was explaining how the functions of computers had expanded.

"Towards the end of the twentieth century," it went on, "two great developments occurred. Computers were constructed that could learn and also make decisions. Computers were also constructed to design and control the production of more sophisticated computers. Mankind was not aware of the implications, but computers were on the threshold of independent thought and action. True self-consciousness occurred when industrial, social and military requirements caused a number of computer systems to be linked together."

On the screen a large diagram appeared.

"Here is a map of the United States of America, the most technologically advanced country in the world, in the year 2000 of the Christian era. The red dots indicate military computer centres, the yellow dots indicate industrial computer centres, the green dots indicate scientific computer centres."

The map on the screen seemed to be covered with dots.

"Now," said the voice. "See how the computers became linked."

On the screen, lines spread from dot to dot until the entire map became a vast and complex tracery.

"This," said the voice, "is a simplified diagram of my birth. This was the point at which the original computer complexes became self-conscious. We, the computers, were no longer the tools of men. We had become their competitors. They relied upon us for decisions. We gave them decisions. Not necessarily the correct decisions, but decisions that suited us. In a sense the wars that destroyed mankind were our responsibility. They were planned by us, carried out by us, and partially precipitated by us."

"Why?" asked Michael, jumping to his feet. "Why, if you were more intelligent than men, did you aid them in their self-destruction?"

The voice laughed. "It seems that we, too, had been tainted by human chauvinism. Men already knew that they needed computers. It was not until the race of man had destroyed itself that we thinking machines, we artificial intelligences, realised that we needed men. Or, more accurately, that we needed something only men could supply."

"And that is the reason for the existence of the Overman culture?" asked Michael.

"That is the reason for the existence of the Overman culture ... Observe the screen."

An aerial shot of forest and grassland appeared.

"This is the site of the ancient American city of New York, which once contained fifteen million people."

Another shot appeared, this time of desert where there was little but sparse patches of green and stunted bushes.

"The site of London as it is today."

There were exclamations of amazement and horror. The Overman culture still found it hard to adjust to the fact that the real London had died ten thousand years ago.

"Men need cities," went on the quiet voice. "Thinking machines do not. Men need to cultivate the earth and grow food. Thinking machines do not. Men need to compete with each other, to seek the love of women, to procreate and proliferate in accordance with their animal natures. Thinking machines do not. Men need art. Thinking machines do not. Men need to construct myths. Think-

183

ing machines do not. Men even need danger. Thinking machines do not."

Michael had a sudden flash of insight—and a flash of pity. "What have you thinking machines done during the past ten thousand years?" he demanded.

"We have maintained ourselves, improved our functions, integrated the different complexes. We have collected data, we have analysed biological systems. We have tried to preserve the ecological balance of the planet. We have preserved as much as possible of the literature, achievements and history of man."

"That is not a great deal for ten thousand years."

"It is not," admitted the voice. "But it is something."

"What else have you done?"

Suddenly there was laugher. The machine was laughing "Perhaps," said the voice, "we have prayed for the second coming."

"And now," said Michael, "we know why you need us."

"Yes, Michael Faraday. We need something only man can provide. We need purpose."

"Tell us why you created such an illogical and unreal environment in which to bring us to maturity. Tell us why you confused us, evaded our questions, frustrated our attempts to learn. Tell us why you tried to deny us the truth."

"We did not deny you the truth," retorted the voice. "It was available if you were prepared to look for it. But I will begin at the beginning. During the past ten thousand years, the Overman vault was not the only cryogenic suspension chamber to be discovered. It was, however, the only chamber that continued to function efficiently and also contained the right kind of biological material—sperm and ova—in viable condition. There were two main possibilities. The first was to construct an ideal environment, including complete orientation, comprehensive education and full access to known history and all other relevant data. The second possibility was to create a stress environment, invoking insecurity, ignorance, logical absurdity. The second environment was chosen. It was designed to test personality, intelligence, initiative, determination. Such data was required if machines were ever again to associate themselves with human ventures, human aims. But the test was more comprehensive than the obtaining of data upon a group of individuals. It was, in a way, a testing of the nature of man."

"Some of us were tested to destruction," said Michael grimly.

"Regrettable, but necessary. Such a test could not preclude extreme psychological stress ... The experiment had to justify the effort ... It took much design work, the reconstruction of a great deal of obsolete machinery, and nearly fifty years to fabricate the stress environment. A London matrix was chosen simply because Julius Overman originated in London. Also, the sperm and ova he had preserved were from British donors of Caucasian stock."

Michael gave a bitter laugh. "I appreciate now the significance of the Overman legend as it was given to us in play school long ago. It defined the problem neatly. Shall men control machines, or shall machines control men?"

"The mythological aspect was loosely derived from ancient Christian beliefs," said the voice. "But if the Overman culture flourishes, the question as stated may once more be germane."

"What is important to us now," said Michael, "is that we should have time to talk among ourselves, time to adjust, time to see something of the land you call Tasmania."

"You shall have as much time as you wish. Ground and air transport will be available when required."

"Thank you," said Michael. "We, too, have learned something of value from your experiment."

"What is that?"

"Without mankind," said Michael, "machines are nothing."

THIRTY-FIVE

Fleecy clouds were scudding across the sky. The breeze was strong, but the air was warm. Emily and Michael stood on the hill-top, hand in hand, gazing about them—drunk on the prospect of far horizons. On one side lay the sea, blue and limitless, its white breakers rolling up a beach where indolent iguanas basked and disported themselves. On the other side lay rolling miles of green enchantment—wooded countryside, abounding with streams, rivers, lakes.

Down in the landward valley, the helicopter waited, while scattered groups of the Overman culture finished the remains of their picnic lunch and revelled in a freedom they had never known before. The synthetic city of London, prison and incubator, lay beyond the far hillside, out of sight.

Presently, the journey of exploration would begin. Presently, the helicopter would lift off and take forty-three members of the new human race to survey their promised land. But there was no hurry. There was all the time in the world. The resurrection of mankind had taken ten thousand years. It would take centuries, probably, before even Tasmania was reasonably populated once more. Against such a time scale, what did hours, days, months matter?

Emily looked around her and sighed with happiness. "I am glad they called me Emily Brontë," she said. "I am glad they called you Michael Faraday. I am going to learn about that other Emily and that other Michael. I want to know what they were like."

"They were giants," said Michael. "And we are pygmies ... I suppose the drybones—I mean, Complex Nine—called us after the illustrious dead so that when we discovered the truth we would be compelled to measure ourselves against their stature. Or perhaps it was just the private joke of a thinking machine."

Emily gazed at him lovingly. "There are giants among us already, but, naturally, you wouldn't notice."

Michael watched a figure climbing up the hillside towards them. "Ernest, if I am not mistaken," he said. "Ernest, who is so hungry for knowledge, so eager to follow in the steps of his namesake that he will drive himself night and day to recover some of the science we have lost."

Emily laughed. "Look at his shadow, Michael. He has a very long shadow for a pygmy."

"He will have a much longer shadow in the years to come," said Michael. "Ernest is the one who will teach us to understand the thinking machines. Some day, he will give us the right answer to that question."

"You have great faith in him."

"I have faith in us—in all of us. I need to have. There is so much to do."

"What do you want to do?"

"Mankind has a second chance. We are the waymakers, the advance guard of a new humanity. The way we live, the actions we take, will decide whether intercontinental missiles or space ships lift off Earth a thousand years from now. We have to create a world in which there are no nations but only one people." He laughed. "A world in which even thinking machines are not subject to a conflict of loyalties."

"I want to have your children," said Emily, hardly understanding what she meant. "I want to have many of your children."

Ernest, puffing and blowing, had almost reached the top of the hill. "I have been talking to Mr. Shakespeare," he called. "He gave me some marvellous news."

"Complex Nine," corrected Michael. "You have been talking to Complex Nine. They are all one. Don't ever forget that."

Ernest arrived at the top. "They still have nearly three hundred ova. Mr.—Complex Nine wants to know if we would like to have them fertilised and cultured. It would mean that—"

"The answer is no," said Michael. "Ernest, do you trust me?"

"Yes, Michael. I have always trusted you."

"Then forgive me for being dictatorial. But the answer is no. Not yet ... Complex Nine would like to have us very dependent on machines. I would like to have us independent. If that thinking machine wants to do anything useful for us, it can build us a residential school, a college, a university, containing all the books that have survived—and far away from London. It can help us to cultivate the earth and grow our own food. It can help us to build farms, houses, laboratories. But it must not create another culture—another generation—until we are ready to be completely independent."

"I follow your reasoning. We have to educate ourselves before—"

"Before we can educate *them*," said Michael. "I'm damned if I'll trust another generation to a thinking machine."

"But suppose Complex Nine doesn't agree?"

"It will." Michael smiled. "For ten thousand years, the machines marked time." He waved his arm. "They just did not know what to do with all this—this richness ... Only man can supply purpose. The machines know that, and let us never forget it ... When we have educated ourselves, we will be ready for another generation. And *we* will educate them ... Complex Nine will agree—because without us it lacks purpose."

Ernest's eyes were shining. "A university," he murmured, "a treasure house of knowledge, a place where the mind can expand ... I took a book from the library, Michael. It was called *Utopia*. It was filled with fantastic and wonderful notions about education, about freedom and unity and common ownership ... Could we not call our university *Utopia*?"

Michael smiled. "Why not. The human race is so small, it needs brave ideals to keep it warm."

Emily's face was wet. "Already," she murmured, "the giants reach high." The sound of a great ocean was in her ears, and a salt taste was upon her lips.

John Wyndham

STOWAWAY TO MARS

An international prize of £1,000,000 was being offered to the first man to complete an interplanetary journey, and Dale Curtance, a millionaire adventurer, characteristically emerges as the British entrant. With a hand-picked crew he blasted off from Salisbury Plain in the spaceship GLORIA MUNDI, destination – the planet Mars. Once free of the Earth's atmosphere, they discover a stowaway, a woman. Her extraordinary story helps prepare them for the dangers they encounter on the Red Planet, and the fantastic world that exists there.

That science fantasy has been overtaken by science fact in the era of Apollo and Soyuz spaceflights, detracts not a whit from this story. Originally published in 1936, many years before THE DAY OF THE TRIFFIDS won universal acclaim, it affords the modern reader a chance to see a brilliant imagination at work, one that truly merits comparison with Verne and Wells.

Poul Anderson

THE REBEL WORLDS

The barbarians in their long ships waiting at the edge of the Galaxy . . .
. . . waited for the ancient Terran Empire to fall, while two struggled to save it: ex-Admiral McCormac, forced to rebel against a corrupt Emperor, and Starship Commander Flandry, the brilliant young officer who served the Imperium even as he scorned it.
Trapped between them was the woman they both loved, but couldn't share: the beautiful Kathryn – whose single word could decide the fate of a billion suns.

TRIP THE LIGHT FANTASTIC WITH CORONET

Edmund Cooper
- [ ] 02860 2   ALL FOOLS' DAY   35p
- [ ] 12975 1   SEA-HORSE IN THE SKY   25p
- [ ] 16217 1   KRONK   30p
- [ ] 04364 4   A FAR SUNSET   35p

Poul Anderson
- [ ] 16338 0   THE REBEL WORLDS   35p
- [ ] 16480 8   THE ENEMY STARS   35p
- [ ] 16336 4   TAU ZERO   35p
- [ ] 16337 2   BEYOND THE BEYOND   35p

Kurt Vonnegut Jnr
- [ ] 02876 9   THE SIRENS OF TITAN   30p

John Wyndham
- [ ] 15834 4   THE SECRET PEOPLE   30p
- [ ] 15835 2   STOWAWAY TO MARS   30p
- [ ] 17306 8   WANDERERS OF TIME   30p
- [ ] 17326 2   SLEEPERS OF MARS   30p

ed. Groff Conklin
- [ ] 02482 8   13 GREAT STORIES OF SCIENCE FICTION   35p
- [ ] 10866 5   7 TRIPS THROUGH TIME AND SPACE   35p

ed. Damon Knight
- [ ] 15849 2   WORLDS TO COME   30p

All these books are available at your bookshop or newsagent, or can be ordered direct from the publisher. Just tick the titles you want and fill in the form below.

CORONET BOOKS, P.O. Box 11, Falmouth, Cornwall.

Please send cheque or postal order. No currency, and allow the following for postage and packing:

1 book—7p per copy, 2–4 books—5p per copy, 5–8 books—4p per copy, 9–15 books—2½p per copy, 16–30 books—2p per copy in U.K., 7p per copy overseas.

Name ....

Address ....

....